"BLOOD WILL RUN," SAID DANCING HORSE.

The warrior's eyes met Kincaid's across the room.

The Cheyenne's features might have been chiseled out of mahogany. He was a proud man whose life had been spent in warring.

"It is pointless to be bitter, and yet bitterness does exist," Dancing Horse said. "Yes, I will follow orders." He picked up his blanket and wrapped it around his shoulders. "Everyone will follow orders, and then there will be blood..."

EASY COMPANY

EASY COMPANY
ON THE OKLAHOMA TRAIL

JOHN WESLEY HOWARD

A JOVE BOOK

EASY COMPANY ON THE OKLAHOMA TRAIL

First Jove edition published February 1982

First printing

Printed in the United States of America

Jove books are published by Jove Publications, Inc., 200 Madison Avenue, New York, NY 10016

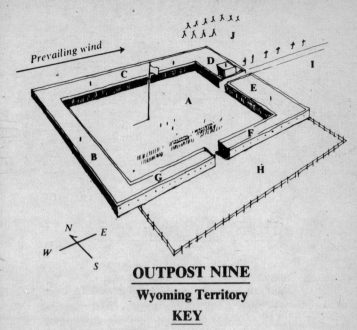

Prevailing wind

J

I

D

C

E

A

F

B

G

H

N
E
W
S

OUTPOST NINE

Wyoming Territory

KEY

A. Parade and flagstaff

B. Officers' quarters ("officers' country")

C. Enlisted men's quarters: barracks, day room, and mess

D. Kitchen, quartermaster supplies, ordnance shop, guardhouse

E. Suttler's store and other shops, tack room, and smithy

F. Stables

G. Quarters for dependents and guests; communal kitchen

H. Paddock

I. Road and telegraph line to regimental headquarters

J. Indian camp occupied by transient "friendlies"

INTERIOR   OUTSIDE

OUTPOST NUMBER NINE
(DETAIL)

Outpost Number Nine is a typical High Plains military outpost of the days following the Battle of the Little Big Horn, and is the home of Easy Company. It is not a "fort"; an official fort is the headquarters of a regiment. However, it resembles a fort in its construction.

The birdseye view shows the general layout and orientation of Outpost Number Nine; features are explained in the Key.

The detail shows a cross-section through the outpost's double walls, which ingeniously combine the functions of fortification and shelter.

The walls are constructed of sod, dug from the prairie on which Outpost Number Nine stands, and are sturdy enough to withstand an assault by anything less than artillery. The roof is of log beams covered by planking, tarpaper, and a top layer of sod. It also provides a parapet from which the outpost's defenders can fire down on an attacking force.

one ——————————

The door to the orderly room flapped open and Sergeant Ben Cohen turned to greet his commanding officer. Captain Warner Conway looked a little ruffled this morning—not that he didn't have the right. There was usually enough going on at Outpost Number Nine, this isolated, undermanned, undersupplied wart on the Wyoming plains, to ruffle better men. If better men there were—an unlikelihood in Sergeant Ben Cohen's estimation.

"Good morning, sir," Cohen said briskly.

"Good morning, Sergeant Cohen."

Captain Conway took the mail from Cohen's desk and walked crisply to his office. Cohen poured the CO's coffee without being asked. He knocked and then entered, placing the cup at the precisely correct spot near Conway's right hand.

The letter from Regiment was in Conway's hands, and he frowned, reread a key paragraph, and shrugged. Cohen, of course, had already read the letter when he opened the mail, but he stood nearby with an expression of polite diffidence.

"Well," Conway said, drumming on his desk. "I guess I'll have to cut Matt Kincaid loose for this project." The captain muttered, "Damn," and placed the letter temporarily aside.

That was all the discussion there would be between Cohen and Conway. The CO knew full well that Cohen had scanned the letter, and now that Conway had voiced his intentions, Cohen would notify Lieutenant Matt Kincaid that his presence was required in the captain's office. They knew each other well, these two strong military men, so alike and yet so different.

Cohen was built like a bear, his temper was hot, and although he was the perfect soldier around Warner Conway, he could be hell on wheels with errant enlisted men.

Conway almost never lost his temper. He was a composed, thoughtful man with handsome, weathered features. Tough as nails he was, underneath, but that facet of his personality seldom showed through.

"There's something you'll want to look at, Ben. Regiment's got nothing better to do than inspect Number Nine again. You've got three days to get ready."

Sergeant Cohen took the second letter and held it. Neither of them remarked further on the inspection. Conway knew full well that Cohen's men were ill-equipped—that they had patched blankets, worn-out boots that wouldn't even hold a shine, that their uniforms were faded and torn—but he made no comment. It was Cohen's responsibility to see that the inspection was passed, and if he knew Ben, somehow Outpost Number Nine would pass with flying colors.

"I'll be damned!" Conway said, slapping his desk with delight.

"Finally some good news, sir?" Cohen asked as Conway read the letter in his hands slowly, smiling.

"John Fairchild's written to me."

"Major Fairchild, sir?"

"The very same. There's a soldier for you, old John. He pulled my bacon out of the fire at Cross Keys. Came riding through a Confederate artillery barrage to pull us out. Old John . . ." The colonel's face was glowing with reverie. "His son's been assigned to Number Nine, Ben." Conway shuffled through the rest of the mail. "Yes, here are his orders. John Fairchild, Jr. There's good news for us, Ben. A sharp young second lieutenant just when we need someone."

"Yes, sir. We won't miss Lieutenant Kincaid so badly, then."

"We'll miss him, Sergeant. Always miss Matt when he's

not around. I wouldn't tell him that," Conway said with a smile. He was fond of First Lieutenant Matt Kincaid. Matt was a professional and a hell of a man. "Better send someone on over to his quarters now."

"I was on my way, sir," Cohen answered.

Captain Conway had tilted back in his leather chair, holding his coffee cup absently. "John Fairchild's boy. I'll be damned. . . ."

Matt Kincaid was with Lieutenant Taylor at the paddock when Cohen found him. "The captain wants to see you, sir," Ben said.

"Oh? Good news or bad?"

"How much good news do we get?" Taylor asked wryly. He stroked the nose of his bay gelding. The bay was coming along nicely after taking a Cheyenne arrow, which had gone completely through its neck.

"I couldn't call it bad news, sir," Cohen answered after considering the question, "but you'll be moving."

Matt lifted an eyebrow and tugged down his hat. Nodding goodbye to Taylor, Kincaid strode with Cohen back across the parade to Captain Conway's office.

"He's waiting for you, sir," Cohen said, and Matt tapped on the doorframe and entered.

"Matt, good morning. Coffee?"

"I'd appreciate it, sir." Matt seated himself at the captain's gesture and waited as the captain found the communique from regiment. Matt scanned it briefly. "Oklahoma?" he asked with surprise.

"That's it, Matt." Conway rose and stood near the large wall map, which he glanced at briefly. "As you know, the Dakota Confederacy tribes are starting to straggle back from Canada. In their minds, it seems, all the fuss over Custer and the Little Big Horn is over."

"Only in *their* minds," Matt put in. It was far from over to the War Department in Washington. That battle had frightened people badly, and overnight had changed the entire Indian policy. They were no longer so sure just who had the upper hand on the Western Plains.

"Most of the captured Indians are being quartered at Pine

Ridge and other similar large reservations," Conway went on, "and there's quite a number of Cheyennes. Too many. Washington has the word that some of these bands, finding themselves on reservations, are talking about picking up the hatchet again.

"There's a medicine man called..." Conway glanced at the letter. "Wovoka. He's actually a Paiute, they say. Wovoka is talking up the Ghost Dance again, and actually has held one ceremony. The longer these Cheyenne are penned up, Matt, the more influence a Dream Singer like Wovoka is bound to have." Conway perched on a corner of his desk.

"So we simply transport them?" Matt asked.

Conway's eyes flickered. "Militarily it's imperative, Matt. The potentially hostile force is growing in size. Many of these people counted coup against Custer at the Greasy Grass. Yes, we're separating them. There's a band of about forty warriors, plus women and kids and animals, under Dancing Horse. You've heard of him?" Matt shook his head. "Well, you'll find out. He's a tough old fox, Matt. Don't underestimate his intelligence."

"I never underestimate any hostile, sir."

"I know you don't, Matt, but be careful. Regiment wants you to escort these Indians to the agency at Darlington, in the Indian Nation."

"That's between the Canadian and the Washita, isn't it, sir?"

"That's right. Just north of the Washita River. Now it's true that the South Cheyenne, like Dancing Horse's people, used to range that far south on their hunts. They tangled with the Seventh under Custer once, along the Washita. Still and all, they are going to make a hell of a fuss about having to leave their homeland and the green north."

"It's understandable."

"It is. But you be careful, Matt. Pick your own personnel. Regiment has indicated that they are sending three Indian scouts to meet you at Pine Ridge, so take that into account. A platoon-sized force, I think, don't you?"

"Yes, sir," Matt sighed, and got to his feet.

4

"This may amount to nothing more than a summer excursion, Matt," Conway said, rising to walk toward his lieutenant, "but it could turn out to be a hell of a mess. Just watch yourself. Please."

"I intend to, sir. Thank you."

Ben Cohen was in the enlisted barracks when Lieutenant Kincaid arrived. The first sergeant was going through trunks, examining saddles, blankets, and weapons, groaning and cursing as he went.

"Something the matter, Sergeant Cohen?" Matt asked mildly.

"You're goddamned right. . . ." Cohen was facing away from Kincaid as he began to speak, and as he came around, his voice broke into rigid courtesy. "Nothing, sir. There's an inspection around the corner, that's all."

"Be nice if they would issue something worth inspecting, wouldn't it?"

Cohen gave the lieutenant a look of gratitude. "You don't know the half of it, sir."

"Anybody want to beat this inspection?" Kincaid asked, glancing around. "I'm herding some Cheyenne down to the Nation. Volunteers accepted."

Private Malone had been hanging back in the corner, as if to fade into the wall. "How's that work, Sarge?" he asked Cohen. "Locked trunks for men not able to stand inspection?"

"That's right," Cohen said.

"Let me be the first to volunteer," Malone said. He grinned, and Kincaid, despite himself, grinned back. Malone was branded as a troublemaker, and had spent more time sewing on corporal's stripes and ripping them off again than anyone could total. He couldn't hold his liquor worth a damn, and when he drank he fought, but there was no liquor along that Oklahoma Trail, and Malone was a top-notch, veteran soldier.

Platoon Sergeant Gus Olsen had just entered the barracks, and he glanced at Cohen, who was still throwing things aside in disgust. Then the sergeant looked to Kincaid.

"I'd like to ride, sir."

"I'd like to have you, Gus, but you're needed here. There's a green officer coming in. Son of a friend of the captain's. He'll need some breaking in."

Wolfgang Holzer was standing rigidly at attention beside his bunk as Cohen tore through the barracks, tossing much he found into a pile that he intended to have burned.

Reaching Holzer's area, Cohen stopped in amazement. The man's bunk was tightly made, his uniform meticulously pressed, his clothes and blankets cleaned and patched, his boots as glossy as obsidian.

"Why can't you all take care of your equipment like Holzer?" Cohen asked in exasperation. "If I had a platoon of Holzers—"

"You'd have the prettiest, most screwed-up platoon in the U.S. Army," Malone said in a slow drawl.

"Button it, Malone," Cohen growled, more because he didn't care for his men popping off in front of officers than for any other reason. After a moment's consideration, Cohen had to admit reluctantly that Malone was right. Wolfgang Holzer was a born soldier—born for the German army—but an overzealous recruiting sergeant had signed Holzer as he stepped to the docks in New York, not bothering to find out, nor caring, probably, whether Holzer could speak English. The man was efficient, respectful, and neat as a pin. But Holzer's uses were limited.

"I'd like to take Corporal Wojensky, if it wouldn't cripple you or Olsen," Matt said to the first sergeant.

Cohen shrugged. "Fine by me. Sergeant Olsen?"

"We'll make do," Olsen said affably.

"I know I'm leaving you short, Sergeant," Matt apologized, but I need some experienced men, and Wojensky can speak the lingo."

"Some." Gus Olsen grinned. "At least 'eat,' 'drink,' and 'want to go to bed with soldier?'"

Cohen stepped outside with Kincaid, after first ordering Malone and Stretch Dobbs to burn the torn blankets and bits of uniform he had stacked to one side.

"So now you'll have two shavetails to mother, won't

6

you, Sergeant?" Matt asked. He stood on the porch, looking out across the parade. Maggie Cohen was just leaving the sutler's store with a parcel. "There's some money spent," Matt said, nodding.

"Knowing that woman," Cohen said with pride, "it's something for the pot or something for me. She's not the sort to throw money around, my Irish girl."

Returning to the former topic, Cohen said, "I don't mind the green ones, Lieutenant. I guess I've broken in half a hundred in my time—that's the way I look at it, that I broke them in. But most men are smart enough to realize that out here it's learn or die. Most of 'em have learned. Mr. Cambury, now, he's sharp as a tack, and eager to learn. Of course, his thoughts aren't always with us."

Matt smiled. Tad Cambury was expecting his bride-to-be in a matter of days, and the young second lieutenant was understandably distracted.

"And I expect this Mr. Fairchild will be the same. An army brat, Point man. His father's a great friend of the captain."

Four Eyes Bradshaw was waving excitedly to Ben from the orderly room, and Cohen excused himself with a few muttered phrases about clerk-soldiers.

Matt watched him go and then turned toward his own quarters. If Cohen had inspection on his mind, Matt was even more engrossed in his own problem.

Oklahoma.

He wondered if someone had already informed Dancing Horse that his people were being taken to the Indian Nation, or if they had left that chore for Matt as well. He knew how the Cheyenne chief was going to take it; he knew there would be resentment and more than a little anger.

He supposed it was a sort of compliment that Captain Conway had chosen him for this job, and not Taylor or Fitzgerald; but then it was a compliment he could have done without.

With a sigh, Matt went into his quarters and began packing.

The enlisted barracks was bustling with activity when

Corporals Wojensky and McBride entered. Malone was busy packing, as was Stretch Dobbs. Holzer was dusting under his bunk, and Rafferty was digging through his trunk.

"They got him," Wojensky announced.

"Got who?" Malone asked, turning, hands on hips. The cigar between his lips was cold.

"Kip Schoendienst. Four Eyes just got the word from regiment."

"From regiment?"

"That's right. A couple of regimental MPs picked him up sitting on a riverbank fifty miles south, holding his head and moaning."

"Christ—regimental MPs. They'll have to court-martial him, won't they, Wojensky?"

"I do believe so," Wojensky said with a shake of his head.

"Damned fool," Reb said.

"What happened?" Private Trueblood was new to the post and had missed out on the episode.

McBride shrugged. "It wasn't much. It happened in town three nights ago. We had a few drinks and Kip had a few more. All of the sudden he hops up and says, 'Yippee! I'm bound for Texas to herd them longhorn steers.' And off he went."

"You let him go?" Trueblood asked, astonished.

"Hell, I was in no shape to stop him. Besides, how in the hell was anybody to know he was serious? I guess he went out, got on his horse, and headed off, singing cowboy songs."

"If he'd straggled in on his own," Malone explained, "or if we'd been able to find the silly son of a bitch, he might've got off with company punishment. Hell, Kip's a good kid. Green, but he's a soldier."

"Regiment has a record of it now," Wojensky said. "The captain'll have to court-martial him, likely."

"He could get ten years. Hard labor!" Trueblood said with a shudder.

"If he's lucky," Malone said soberly.

8

"What's this about an inspection, Gus?" McBride asked.

"Regimental," Olsen told him. "Best start cleaning up now. Everyone else is."

As he said that, Malone shoved his blankets into his footlocker and padlocked it shut.

"Everybody?" Wojensky asked.

"Not Malone. He's going riding to the Indian Nation."

"To be a cowboy?"

Olsen laughed. "No. You'll find out, I expect, Wo. You volunteered for it while you were gone. Lieutenant Kincaid's leading a party of Cheyenne down."

"Shit!" Wojensky sighed. "Well, maybe it beats standing inspection." He looked at Holzer, who was flicking the dust from his spare boots with studious concentration.

"Holzer's going too," Olsen told him.

"Then what in hell's he doing that for? Wolfie!" Wojensky called. When Holzer's head came up, the corporal flipped his hands over, indicating that Holzer should simply dump his gear into the locker.

"Inspection!" Holzer called back with a smile. Then he continued with what he was doing.

"Who else is going?" Wojensky wanted to know.

"You, Malone, Dobbs, Holzer, and Rafferty, as of now. Not you, Reb—Kincaid's hoping nothing comes up that he'll need a bugler for. And what would we do without sweet reveille?"

"Suits me." McBride shrugged. "I get homesick far from Number Nine."

"I thought you were breaking somebody in on that damned horn," Malone said.

"I was." Reb glanced up. "Kip Schoendienst."

The stagecoach rolled on after changing teams at Carmody Wells. Dust streamed out behind the stage, a long, yellowish plume that drifted for half a mile and more across the dry grass plains. The road was dry, and Gus McCrae worked his six horses, making good time. He had only two passengers, both originating at Fort Laramie. They sat facing

9

each other now, one a young man in the uniform of a second lieutenant, the other a frosty-eyed young woman named Pamela Drake.

"Will we make it today, then?" Pamela asked. She held tightly on to the leather strap on the wall of the coach, grimacing with each jolt.

"We should." John Fairchild smiled and once again measured Pamela Drake. He found her worth the measuring. Tall, elegantly dressed in green silk and white lace, with eyes of an extraordinary deep green, her hair was auburn, swept back, and hung with ringlets. Her lips were full and there was a subtle, mocking sensuality to them.

Pamela Drake returned Fairchild's glance for a moment, then turned her eyes to the empty, unbroken land outside. The long grass was flattened by the gusting wind. Far in the distance, Pamela saw a low knoll where a bedraggled, half-dead oak stood. Except for that, the land was as flat as the sea, and as interminable.

"It's a dreadful place, isn't it?"

She looked at Second Lieutenant Fairchild once again. He nodded. A young man of twenty-one, he had closely cropped blond hair that curled against his scalp, and a pale mustache that hovered over a slightly cynical mouth.

"It's a springboard," Fairchild commented.

"I beg your pardon?"

"Simply a place to be gotten through, Miss Drake. May I call you Pamela?" She smiled and nodded. He went on, "For myself I see Wyoming as an opportunity to begin carving out my career. I have a leg up out here," he said with a wink.

"A leg up?"

"Pull, that is." Fairchild shrugged and glanced away. "My old man soldiered with Captain Conway."

"Oh. Is that the way careers are carved out in the army, Lieutenant Fairchild?"

"It's the way they're carved out everywhere, Pamela," he said, leaning far foward, looking steadfastly into those deep green eyes.

"Yes, I suppose so, Lieutenant—"

"Look here, I can't properly go on calling you Pamela if you're going to insist on calling me Lieutenant Fairchild. John, please!"

"All right—John." She smiled and glanced demurely down at the floorboard of the Concord stage. The coach hit another pothole and Pamela was jolted from the seat. She collided with John Fairchild, and his arms went around her.

He picked her up carefully, his hands staying on her waist moments longer than necessary. "Thank you," she said breathlessly, straightening her hat.

"Can't you slow down a little?" Fairchild called out the window, but the coach kept on at the same frantic pace; it was doubtful that McCrae even heard the shout.

"That's all right." Pamela smiled faintly. "I suppose I must get used to all of this. After Tad and I are married, we will spend a lot of years on the plains, I expect."

"I expect so." Fairchild was silent, looking out the window. "Not much of a get-around for a woman, is it?"

"I'm sure I don't expect more, as long as I'm with my husband-to-be."

"No, of course not."

She found herself suddenly fascinated by John Fairchild's hands. The sunlight streamed through the window and illuminated the golden hairs on his freckled knuckles. She caught his gaze on her, and started as if he had poked her.

"I'm sure I don't know what's the matter with me." Pamela patted her curls.

"It's the long ride, the unfamiliar surroundings," he said comfortingly. Yet the gleam in his eyes was hardly comforting. She knew it for what it was; Pamela Drake was used to having men look at her hungrily.

She turned her head away. What *was* getting into her? A bride's nervousness, she supposed. Alone in a strange land...what was she doing here! She closed her eyes tightly. The stagecoach rumbled on.

"All ready then, Matt?" Lieutenant Tad Cambury asked.

"I'm packed," Matt answered. "Ready? I hope so. That's a long trail down to the Nation."

Cambury himself was riding out. He and Fitzgerald were riding night patrols now. There had been some renegade problems on the western perimeter and Conway wanted to make sure the Indians saw blue day and night. Often that was enough to discourage them. So far there had been little real trouble; apparently it was only a few young bucks who had jumped the agency, trying to prove their manhood in the old way. A few cattle had been stolen, a barn burned, but the settlers were demanding patrols, and Conway was forced to oblige them.

Cambury stood at the window, staring off toward the outpost's main gate. Matt Kincaid had picked up his bedroll and his Springfield rifle.

"It doesn't roll in until six o'clock at the earliest," Matt said teasingly.

"I wasn't . . ." Cambury blushed. "I guess I'm a bit anxious."

"Who wouldn't be?" Matt rested a hand on the second lieutenant's shoulder. "I'm only sorry I won't be here for the ceremony."

"I wish you could be. I wanted you to be my best man, Matt. You've been terrific to me. All of you—the captain, Taylor, Fitzgerald. You've made it easy for me. And I know Pamela will love it out here, with all of you to make her feel welcome."

"She will be welcome, Tad, believe me. The captain's lady is looking forward to meeting her. Maggie Cohen has already planned some decorations for your new quarters."

Matt stuck out his hand and Cambury took it with both of his own. His open, ruddy face was thoughtful and happy at once.

"I'll be seeing you real soon, Tad. You'll have me to dinner?"

"The night you return. It's a promise," Tad Cambury said. He walked out onto the boardwalk, into the intense sunlight with Matt Kincaid, watching the flag that fluttered weakly on the pole at the center of the parade.

Corporal Wojensky had led Matt's horse over to them,

12

and Cambury watched as Matt tied on his roll, slung his saddlebags over the bay's haunches, and swung up.

"Don't forget," Matt said. "Dinner."

"It's a promise," Tad Cambury said with a grin. Then he watched as Matt Kincaid trailed out, leading his platoon eastward, toward Pine Ridge.

Cambury stood there a minute longer, watching the dust settle, listening to the sounds of the camp. She *would* like it. He had promised Pamela that, and he would see to it. What he had told Matt was true; having friends like Kincaid and Taylor would make it easy for Pamela to fall into the routine of army life.

He thought of her face, trying to picture it perfectly. Her eyes he could recall vividly, and those alive, incredible lips. The rest somehow faded in memory...no matter, she would be here tonight, tomorrow at the latest, and the chaplain would ride over from Regiment. She would be his wife and they would be happy out here.

He turned back toward the quarters, started to whistle dryly, and broke off, finding his lips dry, his throat tight.

Inside, Cambury began readying himself for the night patrol. He found himself worrying about nothing in particular. It's only a groom's nervousness, he told himself.

She *will* be happy here.

two

It was dusk when Matt Kincaid's party reached Pine Ridge. From the grassy knolls where they sat their horses, they could see cones of fire dotting the broad prairie. Clustered around the fires in the purple haze that settled into the valley were a thousand or more tipis.

"That's a sight," Corporal Wojensky muttered. "I'm damned happy they're 'subdued.'"

"Makes a man realize why Washington is getting a little nervous, doesn't it?" Kincaid commented. "Subdued or not, it's a sight to see. It must be the biggest gathering of Plains Indians since Little Big Horn."

Kincaid's platoon was not the only one in the area. Outside the agency walls, other soldiers were tented up as Matt led his men toward the stockadelike agency building, which stood starkly against the paling sky.

Nightfall had brought a chill, and steam curled from the horses' nostrils. Inside the agency, smoke twisted skyward from twin chimneys.

"Make camp outside the east wall, Wo. Don't cut anybody free. I don't want any Easy Company personnel trying the sutler's beer or the hogtown girls."

"Yes, sir." Wojensky answered. "You going to ride in?"

"I might as well. Get the paperwork done tonight, if possible." He glanced toward the Indian camps. "Tomorrow we'll have other problems."

Matt found the agency office still lighted. It was hardly surprising; managing the hundreds of Indians here, and keeping them supplied, was a large job.

He walked into the outer office, and found it deserted. The clerks, it seemed, were allowed to go home. A lantern burned brightly in the inner room, and Matt walked to the doorway.

A thin, balding man in shirtsleeves sat behind the unfinished pine desk. The light from the wall lamp glittered on the two golden rings he wore, and lent a sheen to his head.

"Mr. Bishop?"

The man glanced up, nodded, and came to his feet. He was not alone in the room, Matt now saw. Sitting erect in a wooden chair in the corner of the room was a Cheyenne of middle years.

"Yes, I'm Bishop. Are you from Outpost Number Nine?"

"That's correct. Lieutenant Matt Kincaid."

Bishop thrust out a clawlike hand and Matt took it, his eyes across Bishop's shoulder on the Cheyenne. "As you might have guessed, this is Dancing Horse, Lieutenant Kincaid."

The two warriors' eyes met across the room. Those of Dancing Horse were not hostile but amused, perhaps slightly contemptuous, but above all intelligent, measuring.

"Dancing Horse." Matt nodded, and the Cheyenne nodded back without speaking, without rising.

The Cheyenne's features might have been chiseled out of mahogany. He was a purposeful, proud man whose life had been spent on the Plains, in hunting, in warring. He wore a white linen shirt and buckskin trousers. His hair was unornamented, hanging in two long, gray-streaked braids across his shoulders.

"Sit down, please, Lieutenant." Bishop gestured and Matt took a chair beside the agent's desk. He lay his hat on an unused corner of that desk, and Bishop went on, "Dancing Horse and I were only now discussing the details of this trek. Both the army and the BIA have agreed that this should be a slow—one might say leisurely—journey.

15

We have women and children in the group, as you know, and there is no sense in exhausting anyone."

"I understand that," Matt said. "I certainly will not be pushing, as long as we make reasonable time."

"Good." Bishop beamed a practiced, professional smile in the direction of Dancing Horse. "I have already informed Dancing Horse that no weapons are to be allowed to remain in the hands of his people, and he has given his word that all weapons will be turned over to you."

"Yes," Dancing Horse said with heavy sarcasm, "since we will not need to hunt, we need no weapons. Since we will no longer be warriors and hunters, but wards of the government, we need not worry about eating. The food will be there and all things will be as they should. Children," he said contemptuously, tossing his head. "We are treated as children."

Matt said nothing in response; there was nothing to say. It was true, the Indians were losing their freedom. Obviously, however, they could not lead a party of forty armed warriors southward.

"You will have weapons for hunting once you reach the Indian Nation, Dancing Horse. Assure your people of that," Bishop said with a wispy smile.

"Yes." The old warrior nodded. "And what is there to hunt in that desert? I am no fool, I know the land called Oklahoma. Indian Nation, you call it! If that is so, may I ask you, do Indians have sovereignty over their own nation? I think not—Indian Nation means 'big reservation,' I think."

Bishop was mildly exasperated. He tapped rhythmically on his desktop. "There's hardly any point in bringing all of this up again, Dancing Horse. I am sure Lieutenant Kincaid is now suitably impressed by your arguments. But," he said, rising, "since the decision has already been made, trotting out old objections seems essentially pointless."

"You are right," Dancing Horse said. "It is pointless to be bitter, and yet bitterness does exist. I only thought Mr. Lieutenant should be aware of that."

"I am sure Lieutenant Kincaid *is* aware of that." Bishop

16

turned now to Kincaid. "You will be well provisioned, sir, but undoubtedly your supplies will need replenishing en route. Therefore I am authorized to advance certain monies against later certified claims." Bishop withdrew a small steel box from the bottom drawer of his desk, and from this he counted out two dozen gold double eagles. "Please make sure expenditures are properly receipted."

"I will, sir," Matt said, signing the voucher that Bishop had shoved across the desk. The agent glanced at the signature, nodded, and replaced his box. "Then the only—" Bishop had started to lean back, smiling. Now he straightened again, his eyes puzzled. He was looking across Matt's shoulder, and Matt slowly turned around.

"Yes?" Bishop asked.

"Mr. Bishop?"

"Yes, correct."

"I am Iron Owl. These two men are my lieutenants. Reporting from Fort Union to escort a party to the Indian Nation." Iron Owl handed Bishop his orders, which he had carried inside his shirt.

Dancing Horse had come suddenly to his feet, and he was livid.

"Crow! They are Crow!" Dancing Horse shouted, as if the very taste of the word were disgusting.

Bishop shook his head worriedly. Iron Owl stood with his arms crossed on his chest. Matt frowned, looking from Dancing Horse to Iron Owl and back. The Crow and the Cheyenne had been enemies since before the grandfather times. To have his band escorted by a group of free Crow was an intolerable insult to Dancing Horse.

Iron Owl was drawing army wages, as were his companions. The contrast between the Crow and the Cheyenne they were to escort was sharp. Iron Owl wore a red silk shirt with silver sleeve garters. He wore a new black hat with an eagle feather and a band of silver conchos. His boots glistened. He wore two staghorn-handled revolvers and carried a new Henry repeater.

Bishop finished reading Iron Owl's orders and looked

17

helplessly to Matt. "I don't know what to say. This is a terrible mistake."

"Tell this man to go," Dancing Horse demanded, pointing a stubby finger at Iron Owl, who regarded the old chief with a sort of condescension. The Crow, after all, were free allies of the victorious army, the Cheyenne the defeated.

Still, Iron Owl was not heartless. "It seems there is a mistake. I know this will be trouble. Yet these are our orders." He shrugged. "I follow orders, as the lieutenant does, as you do, Mr. Bishop. And my orders, as you have read, are that I and my lieutenants will scout trail for Lieutenant Kincaid to the Indian Nation."

"It's inconceivable—" Bishop began. But nothing was inconceivable in government plans, as both Bishop and Matt knew.

"Blood will run," Dancing Horse said, not threateningly but matter-of-factly.

"The Cheyenne is right," Iron Owl agreed, although his tone made it clear that he thought a Cheyenne was seldom right about anything.

"What do you think, Lieutenant?"

"I think we're stuck with the situation," Matt said, "and that we had all better make the best of it."

"No Crow!" Dancing Horse said firmly.

"What can be done?" Iron Owl asked with a shrug. "Those are my orders. Unless one of you has the authority to countermand them." The Crow looked from Bishop to Kincaid and back. He shrugged. "Otherwise, I am bound to follow my orders."

"Dancing Horse," Bishop said beseechingly, "there is no choice here. Someone has made a mistake. But we must all follow orders."

"Yes. I will follow orders." Dancing Horse picked up his blanket and wrapped it around his shoulders. He looked again at the three Crow scouts. "Everyone will follow orders, and then there will be blood," he said ominously. Then the Cheyenne strode from the room, holding his shoulders straight as he passed between the Crow scouts.

Well, Matt thought, *that's a smooth beginning.* To the Crow scouts he said, "We are camped beyond the east wall. Be ready to ride at sunrise."

After sharing a glass of whiskey and some polite conversation with Bishop, Matt himself rode to the camp. There was but one fire, burning low. Most of the men had turned in, but Wojensky and Malone sat near the fire, having a last cup of coffee.

"We set, sir?" Wojensky asked.

"You could say that." Matt told them how it was. "We can expect trouble over this. As a matter of fact, almost any small incident can spark trouble, especially the first few days. They're not thrilled to be going. They're a beaten, proud bunch of warriors."

Kincaid made it plain to them. "I don't want anybody fooling around with the Cheyenne women. That is absolutely out." He was looking directly at Malone, who held his innocent expression. "Report any trouble that may be building, report any weapons. If trouble flares up between the Crow and the Cheyenne, stand back. We leave at sunrise."

There were only a few pale memories of daylight on the high clouds. The wind off the far mountains was cool.

"Had enough of that?" Ben Cohen asked the man in the pit.

"I've plain had it, Sarge," Schoendienst answered. He was up to his shoulders in a six-by-six garbage pit he had been digging since sunrise.

"Climb on out then, *cowboy,*" Cohen said, and Schoendienst did so. He got to his feet, rubbing his sore, dirty arms. "I've got some bad news for you, if you haven't already heard," Cohen went on.

"No, I haven't heard nothin'," the kid said with a faltering smile. "What is it, another hole you want dug?"

"It's not so simple. Put on your shirt, Schoendienst. A report on you has gone to Regiment. That means the TJA will be waiting for the results of your escapade."

"TJA?"

"Trial judge advocate."

"So what's that all mean, Sarge?"

"Dammit, kid, you've screwed yourself is what it means. The captain can't give you company punishment for desertion—not by the book. There are no extenuating circumstances for him to justify going light on you."

"What're you telling me?" Schoendienst asked with growing trepidation.

"What it means is the captain can't look the other way. You put him between a rock and a hard place. It means, Schoendienst, you'll stand a court-martial, and although I doubt they'll shoot you"—Schoendienst gasped audibly—"they damn well might have you breaking rocks for ten years."

"I didn't mean nothin', Sarge. Jesus—I just had a few too many."

"I know it, you silly son of a bitch. I know it, but us knowing it doesn't help matters. Regiment's got this on the books now, Private, and by God I know what's going to happen. The TJA is going to be hovering over the captain. They won't take it too well if he lets you off lightly. It encourages others, Schoendienst."

"Oh God, Sarge, what'll I do?"

"Nothin', boy. You won't do a damn thing. You just sit tight and it'll be done for you."

"Can't you help me, Sarge?"

"If I could, I would. But I can't, Schoendienst. You dug this hole. Now the army's going to shove you in and cover you up."

Schoendienst walked miserably back toward the barracks, and Cohen stood, hands on hips, watching the kid. He was angry with himself and Schoendienst. The kid deserved a kick in the butt, maybe a month in the stockade, but he didn't deserve what he was going to get.

Cohen had seen men who had done ten years. When the army said hard labor, they weren't kidding. It was enough to kill some of them; most came out broken and useless.

Ben looked to the skies, sighed, and walked back across the parade.

Thinking about Regiment got him to worrying about the inspection again, and he was damned if he knew what to do about that, either. Most of those men had blankets you could poke your head through and use for a poncho. Some had boots with soles so thin they left toe tracks when they walked.

That was the army for you. Skinflint Wilson, the post supply sergeant, wouldn't shake loose of any supplies without authorization. And no authorization was forthcoming from Regiment. Yet Regiment expected things to be in-spection-sharp.

He was nearly past the sutler's store before he stopped, his head swiveling slowly around. Pop Evans was leaning on the counter, poring over his books. A few of the troops were drinking three-point-two beer in the back. Over Pop's shoulder, Cohen could see the shelves full of blankets, uniforms, belts and harness, shirts, boots, and shaving gear. The light slowly went on in Ben Cohen's head and he turned away, walking back toward his quarters.

Private Trueblood stepped out of the sutler's, yawned, put on his cap, and stood watching the sky for a minute. Then, moving lazily, he turned back toward the barracks, ready for a night's rest after a day of fire detail and a night of beer drinking.

The officer and the lady came suddenly out of the shadows and were nearly abreast of Trueblood before he saw them. He flagged a salute in the general direction of the officer, and walked on three paces before the voice rang out:

"Private!"

Trueblood spun around. "Yes, sir?"

"Come here."

Trueblood did so. The young second lieutenant waited, slapping his gloves against his hand. The lady beside him— a pretty young thing in a yellow dress and bonnet—smiled as Trueblood stopped before the lieutenant at rigid attention.

21

"What's your name, Private?" Fairchild demanded.

"Trueblood, sir."

"That was a hell of a ragged salute, Trueblood."

"Sir, in the darkness—"

"Did I ask for an excuse, Trueblood?"

"No, sir," Trueblood barked.

"In fact there is no excuse, is there, Trueblood?" Fairchild went on, slowly circling the dismal private. "Tuck in that shirt, Trueblood."

"Yes, sir." The woman accompanying the shavetail giggled, and Trueblood felt his ears growing hot. It was one thing to call a man down, another to humiliate him. Trueblood stood without blinking for a good two minutes before Fairchild turned him loose.

"Let's keep our eyes open from now on, Trueblood," he said in parting. "You're on my list now."

"Yes, sir."

Trueblood held his position while Fairchild, snapping a salute, turned and escorted the lady away toward Captain Conway's quarters. He stood there, listening to the giggling of the woman, an answering low laugh from the officer.

"What the hell was that?" Reb McBride had appeared at Trueblood's shoulder.

"Hell, I don't know. An officer I've never seen before."

"I've never seen him either," McBride told him. "Showing off for the lady, was he?"

"Seems like." They turned back toward the barracks together, Reb glancing back over his shoulder once to see Flora Conway open the door. The light fell onto the shavetail's face and Reb shrugged again.

"Hope that's not going to be a habit with the man," Reb said. "A man like that, he don't get a whole lot of backup from his men in the field. It can get downright hazardous."

Flora Conway greeted Fairchild and Pamela Drake as she greeted everyone—as if their presence cast a saving light across her drab existence, as if life would hardly be worth living if they should have to go away.

22

"But I'm so sorry Lieutenant Cambury isn't on post to-night," Flora said. "It's all my husband's fault. He's just not the romantic he once was, Pamela."

Captain Conway wasn't sure Pamela knew Flora was teasing. He glanced around from the sideboard, where he was pouring drinks for the men in the room, and said, "We really never know when the stage will arrive, Miss Drake. It's been known to be a week late."

"Oh yes, I realize that," she said lightly. "I'm sorry Tad isn't here as well, but he will be soon. And there are so many nice gentlemen here to keep me company in the mean-time."

Conway glanced at Flora. The girl was bubbling, lively, and, it seemed, a little flirtatious for a woman who was about to be married.

Captain Conway handed John Fairchild his drink. Fair-child sat beside Lieutenant Taylor on Flora's prized velvet settee. Beside Taylor, Miss Pamela Drake perched on her chair, and across from her, Flora Conway. The captain remained standing.

"Your father is fine, then, Mr. Fairchild?" Captain Con-way asked.

"Yes, sir. He's in Washington. Where, I suppose, I should be. I understand the promotions are rather slow in coming in the field."

Taylor glanced at Second Lieutenant Fairchild. Well, the man was ambitious. Three months in uniform, and already he wanted to trade his gold bars in for silver.

"A little fighting-army time will give you a sounder base," Conway said. "And that is what we have here at Number Nine. A fighting army."

"That's mostly done with now, isn't it?" Fairchild asked.

"No. Not at all. It is an ongoing defensive action against a highly mobile enemy, for the most part. But we do have our moments, don't we, Mr. Taylor?"

"We do, sir."

Taylor's glass was empty, and he twirled it in his hands. Pamela Drake noticed that and rose quickly. "If you'll allow me, Mr. Taylor," she said. Taylor glanced up with surprise. Pamela leaned across him and took his glass, her breast grazing his shoulder as she did so.

"Why . . . thank you," Taylor said. He looked up to catch Flora's eyes on him. She had seen it too. Pamela Drake apparently liked for men to notice her, and Taylor was sure they did. But he meant to be careful just how much *he* noticed her. She was going to marry Tad Cambury, and in Taylor's book a man didn't fool around with his friend's woman, no matter how available she seemed.

Probably, he decided, he was reading her wrong.

"I've seen our quarters," Pamela said from across the room. "I had hoped . . . my goodness, they're no better than yours!"

Flora nearly choked on her drink, but struggled for and found her reserve, and said gently, "We'll all pitch in, dear, and try to help you make things more homey."

Pamela flounced back to her seat, handed Taylor his fresh drink, and yawned behind a dainty fist. "Excuse me," she murmured.

"Well, it has been a long day for you both, I imagine," Captain Conway said. "Why don't we let you get your rest. In the morning we begin work, John. And, Miss Drake, Mr. Cambury will be here to greet you properly."

Fairchild stood and thanked the captain for his hospitality. He walked to the door with Flora, and waited for Pamela. Taylor stood, but did not go to the door.

When they were gone, the captain poured himself another drink and sat down again. "The boy is the spitting image of old John. And he seems to be sharp as a tack."

"He does, sir," Taylor said, although his own perception of Fairchild was a little less complimentary.

"And isn't Pamela Drake a lovely child?" Flora called from the kitchen.

"Charming. Doesn't seem too thrilled with Number Nine, though, does she?"

"And who is, Warner?" she asked. Flora returned with a cup of tea. She had not offered the men any. It was a

24

waste of time while there was bourbon. "She'll adjust," Flora said. "It takes a time for a woman. For a man too, as far as that goes."

"That it does," Taylor had to agree. "I wish I could see Tad Cambury's face when he finds out she's arrived."

"Young love," Flora sighed.

Captain Conway gave her a look that said, *Old love isn't so bad either, is it Flora?* Flora flushed almost as if he had spoken those words.

Taylor sensed that he was odd man, and he finished his drink without lingering. Then he rose and picked up his hat. "I do thank you for the evening, sir, Mrs. Conway."

"Must you leave, Mr. Taylor?" Flora said in a way that was at once sincere and final. She rose, and Taylor smiled.

"I'm afraid so. There's a lot to do. I'll try to fill Mr. Fairchild in on the area and the hostiles a little."

"Goodnight, then," Flora said. Conway added his good-bye. When the door was closed, he turned to his wife.

"Mr. Taylor does have a deal of tact, doesn't he?" He wrapped his arms around Flora and bolted the door.

It was dark and cool in the room, but he was warm against her. She felt his lips against her throat, felt his hands slip to her hips and draw her to him. Her pulse quickened and a sudden dizziness swept through her.

"I can't," Pamela said, putting her hands on his shoulders.

"No?" Fairchild whispered. "Why not? You want to. You know you do, Pamela."

His lips tasted the lobe of her ear and she felt him growing hard where their pelvises met. She started to draw away, and then, as his lips found her breasts, her resistance flew.

Slowly she unbuttoned his tunic, her kisses eager against his bare chest. "Lock the door," she whispered breathlessly.

"It's locked," Fairchild said. His hands cupped Pamela's full, nearly round breasts through the fabric of her yellow dress. He felt her thrust and sway against him.

"Sure of yourself, aren't you?" she asked.

25

"Cocksure."

She stepped away from him in the darkness. By the faint ribbon of moonlight that leaked through the curtain, he could see her hands move across the bodice of her dress, and in a minute he heard it rustle against the floor.

Another minute, and she had stepped from her petticoats and the moonlight glistened on her voluptuous body. Her hands stretched out to him, and Fairchild went to her, his eyes devouring her, his heart racing.

She sat on the edge of the unmade bed—her marriage bed—and unbuttoned his trousers. Slowly, maddeningly, she undid them, and when they dropped to the floor, her hands caressed his thighs, found his swollen sex. She tilted her head forward and kissed his abdomen. Her hair was soft against him.

"You're no good, John Fairchild," she said. She looked up at him from the bed, her eyes misty in the moonlight. He had to disagree with her.

"I'm immoral as hell. But," he said, leaning forward to whisper into her ear, "I'm damned *good.*"

Pamela leaned back on the bed, drawing him to her. Fairchild kicked off his boots and fell beside her, his lips touching her soft abdomen, her inner thighs, his nostrils filled with her rich, earthy scent.

He kissed her breasts, teasing the prominent nipples with his tongue. He could feel her heart hammering beneath his mouth. Her fingers traveled through his short, curly hair and she held his head lightly to her breasts.

Pamela shuddered, said something quite unintelligible from deep in her throat, and a hand fell away to find his thigh.

Fairchild shifted so that she could cradle his sex in her soft hand. Her fingers moved lightly along the shaft, measuring him, delighting in the touch of this man-thing.

Her thumb traced whorls around the sensitive head of his member, and Fairchild thrust at her hand, his own fingers dipping between her legs to rest in the soft nest of downy hair before finding the rigid, sensitive button of flesh that lay concealed there.

She trembled as he stroked it, and her grip on his man-hood became more demanding. She began to breathe raggedly, and her thighs spread apart to admit his probing fingers, which dipped inside of her, stroking the dewy soft inner flesh.

She turned to him suddenly. The moonlight caught her teeth. Her mouth was slack, her eyes half shut. Pamela shifted and lifted her leg, throwing it across his hips as her hand positioned him.

He felt the warm, moist touch of her soft flesh against the head of his member, and he scooted forward. But she held him back momentarily, tracing slow, maddening ovals with the very tip of his erection.

When he thought that he could stand it no more, she thrust forward with her hips and he felt himself sinking deeply into her. He clutched at her back, her buttocks, drawing her tightly against him.

Fairchild rolled onto his back and Pamela followed him eagerly. He lay watching her, a faint smile on her lips as she swayed against him, her hair falling to his chest, her breasts moving in slow, pendulous rhythm as her hips rose and fell in a demanding cadence.

She fell against him suddenly, her mouth hungrily seeking his, her body trembling and rolling. Fairchild responded hotly, kissing her mouth, her throat, as his back arched and he buried himself in her, his own rhythm coinciding perfectly with hers now.

She pitched and swayed, her breath moist and hot against his ear as their pelvises collided, sparked, and worked frantically toward an onrushing climax.

Pamela went rigid, felt the tiny muscles within her ripple and twitch spasmodically, before she came completely undone, every fiber of her going slack against the man beneath her.

Fairchild stroked her hips, the small of her back. He kissed her mouth again, deliberately, and then he could no longer hold it back, and with a final, frenzied series of thrusts, he came with a rush. A deep, loin-debilitating climax, it left him exhausted, deeply satisfied, and he lay

27

back, stroking her head, which rested against his chest, murmuring sweet, hollow words into her ear.

Taylor stood on the porch before the officers' quarters, looking out across the moonlit parade. The outpost wall cut a dark silhouette against the sky. He could see the night guards walking the parapet. From far off across the prairie, a coyote howled and was answered.

Where was Fairchild? It was his first night on the post, and it seemed unlikely that he would have wandered far. Pop Evans had closed up, and Rothausen's kitchen was dark, so he hadn't stopped in there for coffee.

There was no point in worrying about it, Taylor supposed. John Fairchild was a big boy. But it puzzled Taylor—where in hell could he have gone? Taylor went back in and unmade his bunk. He was sitting on his bed, still thinking about it, when Fairchild made his appearance.

"Hello, Taylor, nice night."

"Hello, Fairchild."

The man got busy making up his bed, and Taylor didn't have to ask where he had been. He could smell it on him all the way across the room. He knew what the man had been up to, but with whom? An unsettling notion lodged in Taylor's mind and he stood and casually walked to the open door, looking across the parade.

As he watched, a light went on in Pamela Drake's quarters—only now went on, although she had been there for over an hour. Taylor hadn't seen a light earlier. He turned back slowly and glanced at Fairchild, who was whistling happily.

"Good night," Fairchild said, shucking his trousers. He turned in and nodded and smiled and rolled over, clutching his pillow.

Taylor did not smile in return. He turned out the lamp and lay awake in the night for a long hour, thinking.

three ────────────────

With the dawn, they were up and moving. The Cheyenne struck their tents and gathered their belongings. The children ran chattering through the camp; to them, it was a great adventure they were embarking upon. Dancing Horse stood aside with several of his warriors. Their faces were dark, grave, and from time to time one of them would turn to glance at the Crow, who sat their horses patiently, the sun glinting on the German silver conchos of their sleeve garters, gunbelts, and hat bands.

"That's going to be a problem, sir," Wojensky said to Matt Kincaid, who was bridling his own horse. When Matt looked up, Wojensky nodded at the Crow scouts.

"I know, dammit. If it were up to me, I'd send them back home. Well," Matt said thoughtfully, "maybe we can at least get out of the shadow of Pine Ridge before it starts up."

He led his horse to where Iron Owl sat with his subordinates. The Crow nodded a greeting.

"No sense in holding up, Iron Owl. Why don't you men get started down the trail? We'll follow you easy enough."

"Good." Iron Owl nodded and spoke to his men. "We will ride south by east for a time"—his hand indicated the direction he meant to take—"to skirt the low hills so the travois can make easy ways."

"Fine. Hold up for noon meal and we'll discuss the trail," Matt told him.

"Good." Iron Owl nodded and kneed his pony forward. Then he did what Matt should have anticipated and hadn't. He led his men directly through the busy camp of Cheyenne, instead of riding around it.

They rode proudly, their silver ornaments shining, lording it over the Cheyenne, their new rifles across their saddlebows, haughty arrogance on their dark, handsome features.

"Oh Jesus!" Matt said in exasperation.

The effect of this arrogant maneuver was obvious. The Cheyenne braves turned and spat or cat-called at the Crow, who sat their horses with utter disdain, not bothering to glance at their beaten enemies.

It was, of course, a deliberate affront, and Matt kicked himself mentally for not anticipating it. It was obvious that the Cheyenne hotly resented it.

"Look at the bastards," Lone Pine said savagely. He looked for a rock to heave at the Crow, but could not find one. "Fancy in white man's clothes, fancy with white man's money. They have no right here. No right!"

Flower was at his elbow, and she stood gazing after the Crow in fascination. Enemy they were, but handsome, proud men with wealth to display.

Lone Pine cuffed her on the side of the head, turning her head around. The girl's eyes sparked. "Why did you do that?" she demanded of her husband.

"You look at them as if they were men. White man's dogs. Riding through our camp."

"And if you had known how to fight," she said saucily, "they would not be here, would they?"

With that, she turned on her heel and Lone Pine's anger mingled with the sting of the girl's words. He glared at the vanishing Crow, then turned his angry eyes to his new wife. Flower shook off his hand as he grabbed for her, and she walked away, her hips swaying with challenge.

She had done more than insult him; she had belittled his fighting ability and, by implication, his manhood. It was a time before Lone Pine turned to follow his wife.

"And perhaps I shall teach you something, little one," he muttered. "You and the dog-Crow."

Dancing Horse had asked for all of their weapons, but he had not gotten them. Even Dancing Horse did not expect that. A man needs his hunting rifle, his knife and hatchet. Perhaps Lone Pine's rifle was not studded with silver nails as the Crow's rifles were, but it shot true and killed as well as any other weapon.

Some of the Crooked Lance Society had their paint on, and as Matt rode through the camp, checking on the progress, they turned their faces to him. These were the elite of the Cheyenne fighting men, Matt knew. These blue-faced men had survived the Sun Dance, survived Custer's rifles. They were proud warriors and took no hand in the preparations. They simply watched, arms folded on their scarred chests, and even knowing they were unarmed, the sight of them sent a chill along Matt's spine and caused the hair on the back of his neck to stand up.

The last Crooked Lance he had met had died nearly on top of Matt Kincaid, his knife upraised, his blue-daubed face twisted with anger and pain. That warrior could have been any of these men.

"High-hattin' the Cheyenne, were they?" Wojensky asked.

"What? Yes, and I didn't like it a bit. I'll talk to Iron Owl at noon."

"Looks like we're about ready to move them out," the corporal suggested.

Matt agreed. Looking around, he saw that the tipis were all packed and rolled. The tipi poles were used as travois to be dragged by horses, and sometimes by dogs.

Kincaid was reminded that the Indians had used dogs for pack animals long before the horse came, and in fact the Cheyenne word for horse was the equivalent of "big dog."

On the travois were packed foodstuffs, blankets, the old, and those too young to walk. The men led out; those who had horses to ride were riding them. The women, carrying huge bundles of hides and blankets, trailed in the dust.

31

The kids ran in circles, screaming and yelling, dogs yapping at their heels, harassing the horses. "Might as well make it official," Matt said. He turned slightly in his saddle and raised his arm to his own men.

"Move 'em forward, Wojensky."

Wojensky saluted and shouted above the din to the troopers. Their positions had been preassigned, and at Wojensky's command they split to the right and left flanks. Malone and Stretch Dobbs pulled drag, and it was as dusty and uncomfortable as riding drag on a trail herd. Malone reversed his scarf and pulled it over his face, tugging his hat low.

"Look!" Dobbs lifted a finger and Malone saw them too. Sitting beside a bundle of goods, four men watched the band of Indians trail past. They did not move even to get out of the way of the horses.

"What in the hell are they waiting for?" Malone puzzled. He rode through the swirl of dust, Dobbs beside him.

The seated Cheyenne had their faces painted red. Two of them had their shirts on backward. Malone rode up and shouted: "Let's get it moving now!"

"Yes!" one of them shouted back, but they sat there unmoving.

"Did you hear me!"

"No!"

Jesus, Malone thought. "It's like talking to Wolfgang Holzer," he said to Dobbs.

Stretch shrugged. "We'd best get them moving, Malone." He looked southward, where the main party was already nearly a quarter of a mile away.

"Look, men," Dobbs said, "we've got to get moving. Dancing Horse has given his word. Soldiers have arrived to take you south. It is time now to go. Move out!"

But they sat there. The four Cheyenne made no move to rise or to reply. Malone rubbed his face in frustration. From down the trail, through the cloud of dust, he saw Wojensky riding back toward them.

"What's up?" the corporal asked.

"Them. They won't move an inch, Wo."

Wojensky looked the Cheyenne over and winked at Dobbs. "Stay down. Do not follow us!" he shouted.

At that the Cheyenne rose, hefting their packs, and away they went, trailing after the tribe. Malone just gawked.

"What the hell . . . ?"

"Contraries, my boy. You must have heard of them," Wojensky explained.

"You mean them fellows that say yes when they mean no, and walk backwards and all?"

"The very same."

"I've heard of 'em." Malone scratched his arm. "Never met up with any of 'em, though. I guess that makes sense— most of the Cheyenne I've met have been fighting me. I guess these boys would want to be friends."

"That's the idea."

"Crazy," Stretch Dobbs muttered. "You mean we got to tell 'em everything backwards?"

"That's the only way to handle them."

"Don't make any sense. What ever give 'em the notion to be like that?"

"That is a long story," Wojensky answered. "Let's not get into it now. I'm supposed to be up at the point. Kincaid's going to wonder where I am."

Malone and Dobbs watched as Wojensky heeled his horse out wide of the trail and circled toward the front of the procession. Just ahead of Malone, the Contraries walked backward, managing to keep up with the rest of the column.

"They going to walk all the way to the Nation like that?" Dobbs asked.

"Looks like it—unless we tell them to." Malone grinned and rode forward a ways. "You men! Keep on walking backwards."

The Contraries immediately turned around and began walking forward. Malone said, "See. Nothing to it."

"Plain nuts," Stretch commented. "I don't get it."

"I know a part of the story on them," Malone told Dobbs. "Bunkhouse talk. This isn't something new with the Chey-

33

enne. It's been going on for a long time. There's a legend that goes along with it."

"Tell me, my man," Stretch said. "We've got the time. It's a long trail."

"A part of it's wrapped up in that." Malone nodded toward a stark black basaltic landform to the west. It appeared to Dobbs to be a volcanic plug like those you saw standing here and there on the High Plains. The harder basalt remained standing while the earth around it had long since eroded away.

Along the flanks of the black hump of rock, there were deep scores, as if they had been cut by tools. "That's Bear Butte," Malone told him. "And them grooves are the claw marks of the Spirit Bear."

Malone settled in the saddle and told the story. "Now this Contrary Society was started in what the Cheyenne call the Grandfather Times—long, long ago. It's all because of this girl who was called Contrary Girl. Named that because she wouldn't mind her mother. Whenever her momma told her to go gather up buffalo chips for the fire, Contrary Girl went off to play. She wouldn't sleep in the women's place in the lodge, wouldn't wear dresses.

"Finally her mother got fed up with all this contrariness and threw Contrary Girl out of the lodge one night. She was stolen by Owl—old Owl, he sometimes stands for Death in these Cheyenne tales, you see, so maybe the girl died from being left outside. I don't know.

"Anyway, Owl took her home to be his dinner, but he got fascinated with the girl's ways and he decided to marry her instead.

"Of course, as soon as Owl put forth that notion, Contrary Girl, being the way she was, refused. She snuck away from Owl in the middle of a rainstorm and went to live with Hawk, the war god. Seems she wanted to become a warrior, since she was a woman."

"Still contrary," Dobbs put in.

"Right. Well, Grandfather Hawk said it was wrong and wouldn't never work out, but Hawk, he married the girl anyway. He gave her weapons and paint and treated her like a brother."

"That couldn't have worked out," Dobbs guessed.

"No, it sure didn't. Hawk loved the girl, but he needed a squaw to do his quillwork, to jerk his buffalo meat, to cook, and Contrary Girl wouldn't do none of that. Doubt she went to bed with him," Malone added as an afterthought.

"Doubt it," Stretch agreed. "I don't see how he'd go about getting her to do it."

"I don't either," Malone said. "So, being fed up with the whole thing, Hawk flew her home to her tribe. She was all grown up now and beautiful, but of course still contrary as hell."

"I've known a few women like that."

Malone nodded and went on, "Young warriors came around to court her, playing love songs on their nose flutes, bringing gifts of new blankets and horses, but she turned them all down. There was a passel of them that tried: a heap brave Sioux, a rich Crow, a kindly Arapaho—even a white mountain man—but none of them suited Contrary Girl. Or maybe none of them asked her in the right way.

"One day a tall stranger arrived. He rode a black horse and dressed all in black but for a silver sun-emblem he wore around his neck. He was a sinister-looking fellow, and Contrary Girl's mother didn't trust him a bit. But he was a good hunter and had many horses, and Contrary Girl married him. They rode off together to a high mountain camp.

"He treated her good, but he didn't take her nonsense. She had to do exactly what he told her or he would beat her. The most important thing, he told her, was that she was never to turn her back on him—bad medicine, you know.

"Well, she minded him for a time. But Contrary Girl hadn't changed that much, and it bothered her—why couldn't she turn her back? So one day she did, deliberately, and she heard a growl that sent ice down her spine. When she looked back over her shoulder, she saw that her husband was a Spirit Bear."

"Spirit Bear?"

"Yes sir. There's certain spirits that change into a man—or maybe men who somehow change into animals. But her husband was one of them, and if you took your eyes off him, he turned into a big old silvertip grizzly.

"She took off out of that camp, I tell you. Hawk had taught her how to run like a man, and run she did. But the Spirit Bear just loped along behind her, and pretty soon she got tired.

"He caught her right over there," Malone nodded, "at Bear Butte. He closed in on her with blood in his eyes, and Contrary Girl screamed out for help from the Great Spirit. His claws was reaching up for her just as the Great Spirit took pity on poor old Contrary Girl.

"Spirit Bear struck out at her, but Bear Butte started to suddenly rise, lifting the girl up out of his reach. That's what caused those grooves in the rock there."

"Does look kind of like bear-claw marks," Stretch had to agree.

"Now then, she was stuck up there for an entire winter, with Spirit Bear snorting and pacing below her. Damned if she didn't have a baby up there, all alone—Spirit Bear's get.

"Spirit Bear saw it and he went off, not wanting to kill his suckling son's mother. Contrary Girl got off of the butte as quick as you please and ran for home. She changed after that experience, and married a man and was a good squaw, doing her work, minding her husband.

"But her son grew up as contrary as she had been, and every son of his was the same. Ever since, all the descendants of Contrary Girl has come out the same way, doing everything backwards."

They rode silently in the dust for a few minutes, and Stretch pondered it. "You know, Malone," he said finally, "they ain't really so much more contrary than a lot of white men I know—only difference is they got a better excuse for it."

36

Malone laughed. "You're right there, Stretch, you really are.... What's that?"

"Where?"

Malone lifted a finger. He saw a patch of blue against the brown of the long grass in a nearby swale. "Looks like somebody dropped something. Hell no, it's moving. Somebody fell out."

"A Contrary?"

"Maybe. Or maybe somebody sick." Malone swung his horse that way. "I'll have a look-see."

The wind was brisk out of the north. A few high-stacked clouds emblazoned the deep blue sky. There was someone under that blanket, and as Malone rode up, a face appeared from behind it—a very pretty face.

Malone halted his bay. The horse sidestepped nervously and Malone patted its neck. The girl was no more than nineteen, with huge brown eyes and a handsomely boned face. She glared up haughtily at Malone, her lips pressed into a sullen pout.

"You're getting pretty far behind," Malone told her.

"I don't care!" She jerked her shoulders defiantly.

"Well..." Malone glanced around. "You take care of whatever business you've got and catch up, all right?"

"I am not going. I will sit here." She tilted her nose skyward and turned her head away. Malone removed his hat, wiped his sweatband, and replaced it.

"You've got to go, woman," he said.

"I do not."

Contrary Girl herself, he thought. "Look, uh... what's your name?"

"I do not have to tell you."

"Well, don't then, dammit!" Malone snapped.

The girl was silent, looking downward. The wind moved the long grass around her.

"Spring Walk," she said so softly that Malone could hardly hear her.

"What?"

"My name is Spring Walk," she said loudly. Her eyes locked challengingly with his for a moment, and then fell away.

"All right, Spring Walk, why don't you want to go?"

"It is not your concern."

"The hell it ain't! I'm responsible for you. If you won't tell me, maybe I'll just pick you up and deliver you."

"If you touch me, I will cut your throat."

He looked intently at her. "I believe you would," he said in an undertone.

"So leave me alone."

"I can't do that, Spring Walk. But maybe if you told me what the trouble is, I could help."

"The trouble is Two Fingers!" she said, as if it were self-explanatory.

"Ah, now I see." Malone grinned and she turned her head away saucily.

"Don't mock me, Blue Sleeves."

"Malone."

"Malone?" she asked. He nodded. "Go away, *Malone!*"

"Not until you tell me about Two Fingers," he said, and he swung down from the saddle to crouch beside her.

She sighed in irritation. "I hate him."

"Two Fingers?"

"Of course!" She turned her face to his, and again Malone was forced to notice how beautiful she was. "My father will make me marry Two Fingers. And I do not want to."

Malone shrugged. "So don't."

"I cannot disobey my father. And so I will stay here. I will sit beside the trail and starve."

"I'm damned if I don't believe you're stubborn enough to do it." Malone looked uneasily up the trail. He could make out nothing but dust now. The lieutenant was going to be sore as hell if he didn't get moving. "But you don't have a thing to worry about, Spring Walk."

"What do you mean?" she asked, her eyes dubious.

"Why, once you get to the Indian Nation, the white laws apply," he lied. Malone tilted his hat back. She watched him with cautious appraisal.

"What do you mean?"

"Why, just what I said. Everything has changed now, you know. Down in the Nation, everything will be different. It'll be white law, and under white law a woman don't have to marry a man if she don't want to."

"You do not speak the truth," she said, her eyes shifting, studying him intently.

"Sure I do. Think I don't know?" he laughed. "Why, I'm a white soldier, ain't I? I sure know the laws."

"It *is* true?"

"Sure is." Malone stood. "See, going down that Oklahoma Trail ain't all that bad. Fact is, it's like a road to freedom for you."

Malone was aware now of a lone rider appearing through the dust, heading toward them, and he cursed silently. *Kincaid'll be all over my butt.*

The girl shook her head as if trying to lodge the new idea in her mind, and then she nodded sharply. "I believe you. And so I shall go."

"You're a smart woman," Malone said. He stuck out his hand and the girl took it to rise.

Malone had just gotten her to her feet when he was aware of the horse thundering down on him. He started to turn, and the body of a man slammed into him as the horse galloped past.

Malone and the Cheyenne went down in a heap. The breath was driven out of Malone, but he was aware enough to keep moving.

He wriggled out from under the Cheyenne and spun to face him, coming to his feet. The man was bare-chested, built lean and tough, and he had a knife in his hand.

Spring Walk shrieked something Malone did not understand, and then the Indian lunged. Malone turned sideways and felt the blade of the Cheyenne's knife slice through his shirt.

He kicked out as the Indian drove past him, digging his boot in behind the warrior's knee, and the man howled, buckling up.

The brave pitched forward and Malone, from the corner

of his eye, saw two blue-clad horsemen racing toward them. He glanced at Spring Walk, who stood with her fingers to her lips, staring at the Cheyenne.

Looking closely, Malone saw that the man had only two fingers on his left hand. He had the full complement on his right, however, and he had the knife to augment them. The man was crouched, eyeing Malone with silent fury.

"Stay down," Malone told him. He slipped the revolver from his holster and repeated it, gesturing with an open hand. "Stay down."

But Two Fingers wasn't about to be pacified. He leaped to his feet, cutting at Malone with the long, murderous blade of his knife.

Malone drew in his stomach and skipped back. Then he stepped in again and brought his pistol down hard on Two Fingers' wrist. He heard the sound of bone cracking, watched anguish paint Two Fingers' face. The knife dropped to the earth and Two Fingers went to his knees, gripping his broken wrist.

Wojensky and Lieutenant Kincaid were there, running from their horses. But it was all over. Malone hovered over an injured Cheyenne warrior, gun in hand. Behind him, a pretty, haughty young Indian woman stood watching.

Kincaid was to Malone in another three steps, and he shouted, "Put that damned pistol away!"

"He jumped me, Lieutenant."

"Put it away, Malone. Jesus Christ! What are you up to?" He looked from the beaten Cheyenne to the girl who had moved up to stand nearer to Malone, and then he cursed slowly, silently.

Three hours on the trail, and he had one of his men in a fight with a Cheyenne over a woman. How in hell were they going to make three long weeks on the Oklahoma Trail?

From the look of savage hatred in Two Fingers' eyes, Kincaid guessed Private Malone was not going to make it at all, if the Cheyenne had his way.

four ―――――――――――――

It was still early. There was frost on the ground in the shade, but the sun was shortening the shadows already, a flattened orange ball as it emerged from the long, low line of the horizon.

A horse nickered from the paddock, and the hammer rang against the anvil in the smith's shop. The perimeter guard had been changed, and those who had been out all night were straggling toward the barracks or the enlisted mess.

Second Lieutenant Taylor paused uncertainly before Captain Warner Conway's door. He glanced around almost furtively, and then, inhaling deeply, he rapped. It was two minutes before the door was opened, and then it was by Flora Conway and not her husband.

"Why, Mr. Taylor," she said, as if the early intrusion delighted her. She was still in a nightrobe, but her hair had been brushed and pinned, Taylor noticed.

"I'm sorry to bother you so early, ma'am. Is the captain up?"

"Up and gone, Mr. Taylor. He decided to have breakfast in the mess hall. Sergeant Rothausen does have a tendency to slip once in a while if Warner doesn't make his occasional appearance."

Taylor frowned and looked toward the mess hall. Across the way, Reb McBride had emerged to blow reveille. Flora noticed Taylor's concern.

"Can *I* help you, Mr. Taylor?"

"No, I don't think so." Taylor licked his lips. "Or maybe yes—I don't know. Maybe you are the one I should speak to, If you have a moment."

"Always. There's coffee left, Mr. Taylor," Flora said, stepping back from the open door.

"If you don't mind." He went in and stood fidgeting with the collar of his tunic, turning his hat in his hands.

"Here you are." Flora gave him a cup of coffee and seated herself with a sigh. Taylor remained standing, and she smiled up at him. "Now what was it, Mr. Taylor?"

"Mrs. Conway, it's—I don't even know if I should be saying anything to you. To anybody. But I stayed up half the night over this. . . ."

"Is it, by any chance, about Mr. Fairchild and Miss Drake?" Flora asked, cutting through Taylor's stammering.

He lifted a surprised eyebrow. "How did you know that?"

"I was up half the night worrying about it too," she said. "And I too wondered if I should keep my nose out of it, or speak to Warner, or what exactly."

"How could you know? Are we talking about the same thing, ma'am?"

"I believe so." She sipped her coffee and smiled distantly, quickly. "After you left last evening, I got to thinking that Pamela probably wouldn't be able to get a fire started in that old stove; I didn't even know if there was wood in there. I thought I'd take her some extra blankets.

"She was already in bed when I got there," Flora said, lifting her eyes to Taylor. "I heard some . . . distinct sounds coming from her quarters."

"Yes," Taylor said, "that's it exactly. So do we butt in? The last thing I would do, of course, is to tell Tad Cambury. But if this continues, Tad might find out, probably will. Then," Taylor said, shaking his head, "someone could get killed, Mrs. Conway."

"What of speaking to Mr. Fairchild?" Flora asked.

"I've got the feeling words would have as much effect on Second Lieutenant Fairchild as peashooters do on buffalo, ma'am."

"Seriously?"

"I think so," Taylor said. "He strikes me that way."

"Well, that leaves it up to me, then, doesn't it, Mr. Taylor? If we agree something should be done and we can't speak to Fairchild or Cambury, then," she said, rising, "it must be to Miss Drake that we broach the subject. That must properly be my job. Although," she added musingly, "I don't suppose it will make me her favorite person either."

"I'm sorry to lay this on you," Taylor said. "I just didn't know what else to do." He placed his cup down on her round mahogany table and pulled his hat on, hearing reveille echoing across the outpost.

"Nonsense, Mr. Taylor. It was a burden I already carried. I'm only happy to share it with someone. Do you think Warner should know?" she asked as she escorted him to her door. "Fairchild is the son of a dear old friend."

"Yes, I think he should know. If you don't want to discuss it with him, I will."

"Yes, you're right, of course. I'll speak to him, Mr. Taylor. It's potential trouble—he has the right to know."

"He does, ma'am." He had stepped out onto the porch when he added, "I only hope no one else knows."

"Oh dear!" Flora said softly. She touched her throat with her fingertips. "You don't suppose Mr. Fairchild is the sort to tell about it himself, do you?"

"I'm not sure what kind of man he is, Mrs. Conway. I think he's smarter than that. I hope so. Because he's got the knife in his hand—and the chance to cut his own throat."

Taylor said goodbye and turned back toward the captain's office. Coming up the boardwalk, he saw a smiling, whistling Private Dawkins. The orderly had an armful of blankets, but managed a salute anyway.

"Morning, sir!" Dawkins said cheerfully.

"Blanket day, is it?" Taylor asked.

"That's right, sir. Got to air 'em out now and then. Need your boots polished, sir?"

"No, but you could see if you can clean and press my other trousers."

Taylor slipped a hand into his pocket and found a quarter,

which he handed to the orderly. Personal services such as Dawkins performed for the officers in BOQ were voluntary and paid for. Taylor knew that Dawkins had a large, poor family at home, and he also knew that Dawkins was a regular beaver. Some of the enlisted men scoffed at the orderly job, but Dawkins turned to it with a vengeance.

Dawkins saluted again—a feat with an armful of blankets—and walked, whistling, toward the bachelor officers' quarters.

Taylor had started on when he heard the sound of horses and saw the gates swing open. Fitzgerald and Tad Cambury were leading their platoon in from night patrol. Taylor stood, squinting into the early sun, and then strolled over that way.

McBride had blown grub call, and the men coming in off patrol lifted their heads as one man, eagerly anticipating a hot meal.

Dawkins had hesitated a minute to watch the incoming patrol, and then he reached around his stack of blankets to open the BOQ door.

He stepped in, still whistling, and then broke it off, finding another officer in the barracks.

"Good morning, sir," Dawkins said, greeting the lean, blond second lieutenant.

"Good morning, Private," Fairchild answered stiffly. He was standing at the mirror, his face lathered, razor uplifted.

Dawkins got to his work, stripping Taylor's bed, and then those of Cambury, Fitzgerald, Kincaid, and Fairchild in turn.

Fairchild shaved in a leisurely fashion, apparently not worried about breakfast. He dabbed the extra lather from his chin with a towel, which he tossed carelessly on the floor. Dawkins simply glanced at it and then got back to his work.

"Shine my boots first, will you? Fairchild said abruptly.

"Can't do it now, sir," Dawkins told him. He was folding a corner of Fitzgerald's blanket under the mattress. "But if you'll leave them—"

"I can't very well leave them, Private. I'm going to wear

them." Fairchild's expression was one of pained superiority.

"Then I can't do it. Sorry, sir." Dawkins tucked in Fitzgerald's fresh blanket and moved to Taylor's bunk.

Dawkins had spread the blanket and was smoothing it when Fairchild's boot landed square in the middle of the bed. Dawkins glanced up to see Fairchild's taut face.

"When do you expect Lieutenant Taylor to use his bunk next, orderly?"

"Sir?" Dawkins rubbed his hands nervously on his trouser legs.

"I said, when do you expect Mr. Taylor to use his bunk again?"

"Tonight, sir," Dawkins said in puzzlement.

"That's correct, Private. But I am going to wear my boots *now*. I want them shined."

"I would do it for you, sir, I truly would, but I've hardly got the time. With regimental inspection and all coming up—"

"That's an order, dammit, Private! Haven't you got a brain in your dim skull? I want it done now."

"Sir—" Dawkins nodded slowly and stood. "My shine kit's in the barracks. I'll get it."

The door to the BOQ opened, and Dawkins and Fairchild both looked that way. Sergeant Gus Olsen nodded good morning and told Dawkins, "better get a move on. I want to go over the inspection preparations, Dawk."

"Be right over, Sergeant."

"You'll have to excuse Dawkins from that meeting, Sergeant," Fairchild said as Olsen turned away.

"Sir?" Olsen's head swiveled back.

"Private Dawkins is going to shine my boots first, Sergeant."

"I'm afraid he'll have to skip you this morning, Mr. Fairchild."

Fairchild took three strides toward Olsen. "*Miss* me! Are you countermanding my order, Sergeant?" He managed to say *sergeant* as if it were a derogatory term.

"No, sir," Olsen said. He looked flatly at the young

officer. "I could not, would not countermand a lawful order. But then, as the lieutenant is apparently not aware, it is illegal to *order* any man, orderly or not, to shine your boots or perform any personal service."

"Now you're telling me military law."

"I was simply reminding the lieutenant," Olsen said, fighting to keep control of his voice. "I thought perhaps you were not clear on the point. I do have eighteen years experience—"

"Oh yes! The old sergeant." Fairchild scoffed. He turned back to Dawkins, who was trying to become invisible. "Slap a shine on these, orderly."

"Sergeant?" Dawkins asked desperately.

"You don't have to look at him, Private. I've given you an order!" Fairchild's pale face had turned crimson. The muscles in his cheek twitched.

"Get on back to the barracks," Gus Olsen said, nodding his head toward the door.

"Dammit, Sergeant, I'm warning you!" Fairchild's voice was trembling. The finger he leveled at Gus Olsen wavered. "This is rank insubordination."

"No, sir, it's not. Your order, as I reminded the lieutenant, is unlawful."

"I'll have your ass, Sergeant. By God, *you'll* be shining boots when I'm through with you."

"I don't think so, sir," Olsen said. "Shall we take it to the captain?"

Fairchild was livid. "And whose word do you think he would take, Sergeant? That of an enlisted man or mine?"

"Knowing the captain, sir, I believe he would listen to both sides with an open mind. Now, if you will excuse us? Private Dawkins?" Gus nodded again, and Dawkins scuttled toward the door, leaving his blankets where they sat.

Fairchild's voice roared as Olsen turned sharply and followed Dawkins out. "You'll be sorry, you son of a bitch. You'll be damned sorry, Sergeant!"

Gus Olsen felt his arms quivering with restrained anger.

He strode rapidly away, twelve paces, before he allowed himself to mutter, "Yes, sir. Fuck you very much, sir."

Then he took a deep, deep breath and strode across the parade toward the enlisted barracks, feeling Lieutenant Fairchild's eyes burning holes in his back.

Captain Conway stood with his hands clasped behind him, looking at the map of Wyoming Territory that hung on his wall, without really seeing it. At the rap on the door, he came around.

"Come in," he said.

"Good morning, sir," Taylor said.

"Taylor." The captain nodded, and from his tone, Taylor knew something was troubling the man.

"If you're busy—"

"No, not at all." Conway smiled. "Have a seat. I'm simply mulling over a problem. A disciplinary problem."

"Oh?" Taylor formed a quizzical expression. He sagged into a chair and waited for Conway to elaborate. When the captain said nothing more, Taylor nudged him: "Can't be Malone again. He's gone."

Conway half smiled. "No. But it's alleged insubordination. An enlisted man displaying arrogance to an officer."

"Unusual." It was. Taylor's forehead furrowed. "Care to reveal the particulars, sir?"

Warner Conway sighed. "Well, the complaint was made by Mr. Fairchild. Seems one of our men was ragging him. Disrespect, failure to observe military courtesy."

"Who was the complaint against, sir? If I may ask."

"Gus Olsen."

"Gus Olsen!" Taylor almost laughed with astonishment. If there was any man on the post who was more military, more reliable and affable, Taylor didn't know him.

"That's what makes it slightly incredible to me, Mr. Taylor. I hate to doubt an officer's word, but Gus Olsen, insubordinate!" He waved a hand in disbelief and took his chair behind his desk.

"I can't believe it, frankly," Taylor said.

"I can't either. But I hate to question Fairchild's integrity."

Taylor was silent, juggling his thoughts. Finally he decided to lay it on the line. "There's something else, sir, which may have some relevance to this matter. It too concerns Mr. Fairchild. I hate to bring it up—"

Conway's eyes lifted suddenly to the door, and Taylor looked around to see Fitzgerald and Cambury enter.

"Any trouble?" Conway asked first.

"Quiet as Christmas, sir," Fitzgerald answered. "Saw some tracks, nothing else."

"Fine, fine." Conway smiled at Cambury. "I guess you've heard by now that there's a surprise waiting for you, Cambury."

"I have heard something to that effect, sir," Cambury replied, blushing slightly.

"We'll keep this session brief, Tad. Taylor had one item he wanted to bring up, and then we'll debrief."

Conway looked expectantly at Taylor, whose face was suddenly blank. Taylor looked at Tad Cambury and then at the captain.

"It was nothing, sir," Taylor said, looking at his feet. "It can wait until later."

"This is a serious charge. Very serious. It jeopardizes our entire relationship with these people."

The sun was to Kincaid's back, leaving his face in shadow, but Malone could read the lieutenant's expression well enough by the tone of his voice.

"The warrior—this Two Fingers—complained to Dancing Horse and Dancing Horse brought it to me personally."

"Sir," Malone said, spreading his hands pleadingly, "it wasn't—"

"In a minute, Private Malone." Kincaid shook his head. "According to Two Fingers, you were molesting his bride-to-be. You took her from the column and proceeded to drag her into a ditch, where he came upon you. Now then," Kincaid said, "you may reply."

"Yes, sir." Malone's voice was a low grumble. He sketched in the events, speaking in an impatient shorthand: "Girl fell out. I found her. She didn't want to go along, because she wanted to get away from Two Fingers. I was trying to persuade her to return to the column when the Cheyenne jumped me. He tried to cut me and I broke his wrist for him."

"I believe you."

Malone glanced up dubiously. Kincaid went on.

"But I have to listen to both sides, Malone. I have to give the appearance of impartiality. If the Cheyenne believe I will automatically side with my soldiers against them, I lose their respect. I cannot do that and maintain control. And," Kincaid added, "I do intend to maintain control."

"It was purely a misunderstanding, sir. You could ask the girl how it was. The Cheyenne lost his temper, thought I was bothering his woman. It won't happen again—I'll stay away from him."

"Good. I was going to suggest just that." Kincaid looked across the small park where they had camped. The Cheyenne were again making ready to travel. A dogfight had begun in the middle of the camp, and a woman hurled a rock at the two animals, breaking it up with a howl of protest. One of the dogs limped away.

"The other thing, of course," Kincaid said, "should go without saying. If it does not, allow me to state it clearly. Stay away from the woman, Malone. And all the women. It's the surest way to avoid trouble."

"I mean to, sir, don't worry."

"All right." Kincaid turned away and Malone shrugged.

Malone slipped the bridle on his bay and walked it to the river. The morning sun was dazzling against the slow, silver current. The bay lowered its muzzle and drank.

She appeared from out of the willow brush, and Malone took an involuntary step backwards. He glanced around

49

quickly, but there was no one else nearby.

"You best get away, girl. I'm already in trouble over you."

"I know. I am sorry. That dog, Two Fingers, lied to save face." She smiled and strode toward him as she talked, her legs shifting the buckskin shirt she wore, her hips swaying deliberately.

"Well, that's over. But I can't talk to you. Lieutenant's orders. He'll have my hide."

"Well, then we will not talk." She had stopped a scant foot away from him, and Malone could smell the fragrance of yarrow soap and lilac on her. Her face—bright, pretty, and flirtatious—was turned up to him.

Malone felt his pulse pick up a little. Nervously he glanced around. If anyone saw him, he was sunk.

"Listen, you scoot now, you hear?" he told Spring Walk.

"For now, yes." She moved even closer. She was only inches from Malone now.

She smiled and turned away, looking across her shoulder, her dark eyes sparkling.

Malone muttered, "Christ!"

She was a delight to look at—how long since he had had a woman? After all, what could they do? Plenty. But he watched the swaying of her hips as she walked back up the slope toward the camp and his resolve faltered. She was worth six months in the stockade.

Malone glanced skyward, cursing a nature that had made women a need and a danger at once. If Kincaid ever found out. . . . And then he saw the other man. He had been lurking in the willow brush, and as he moved, a pair of butcher birds, startled, took to wing. It was Two Fingers. He had been sitting there, watching.

Now he looked at Malone for a long minute, his dark eyes savage and murderous. And then the Indian was gone, and Malone was left with his horse and his muddled emotions.

"What's up, Malone?"

Malone glanced over to see Stretch Dobbs leading his saddled horse. Malone only shrugged.

"I saw the woman," Dobbs said with faintly malicious glee.

"Don't even mention it," Malone said. Thoughtfully he went on, "Damn pretty, though, ain't she?"

"She is." Dobbs hovered over him, his six-foot-seven frame casting a long, narrow shadow. "And there's more than one pretty woman around."

Malone frowned at Dobbs and waited for an explanation, but none was forthcoming. Stretch simply winked broadly and stepped into leather.

"See you later, Malone," he said. Then he turned his head and rode slowly away, whistling.

Malone led his horse back into camp, and Wojensky walked over and called up, "Take the right flank, Malone. You and Holzer. We're leaving in fifteen minutes."

"Good," Malone grumbled. At Wojensky's curious glance, Malone explained, "The sooner we ride, the better. I figure as long as I stay on my horse I can stay out of trouble."

They traveled slowly southward. They were into good grass now, and it kept the dust down. Ahead, the Bighorn Mountains loomed against the deep blue sky. They scattered a herd of pronghorn antelope, which went bounding away, flashes of fluid muscle, fawn-brown and white.

It was after noon when Dancing Horse, riding a smallish, deep-chested paint pony, rode up beside Matt. Kincaid nodded and Dancing Horse merely lifted a finger in response.

Turning his head in the direction Dancing Horse indicated, Matt saw a fair-sized herd of buffalo grazing their way almost parallel to their own trail.

"It occurs to me," Dancing Horse said, crossing his arms so that he rode without hands, only the slight pressure of his knees guiding his pony, "that here is an opportunity."

"An opportunity," Matt repeated dubiously.

51

"Yes. Nature provides her gifts."

"The buffalo."

"Yes, the buffalo. Most sincerely." Dancing Horse waved a hand with a grand flourish. "The bread of my people, a friend to my people for centuries."

Matt waited patiently. Dancing Horse had a way of circling his points elaborately before pouncing on them. The Cheyenne leader spoke deliberately now.

"There is food, and the food my people prefer. Why waste army gold on other provisions? Why, to hunt would lighten our hearts! You would be well respected if you would consider the hungry eyes of my men who wish to hunt the buffalo, to perform their ritual of survival."

"No hunt," Matt said simply.

"You cannot have fully considered, sir." Dancing Horse wasn't about to give up. "Why, think of the gold saved. You would do the army a service. Think of the morale of my people—a people straggling toward an unknown land, leaving all the familiar ways behind on this trail of sadness."

"No hunt." Matt watched the buffalo himself for a time. Dark, almost prehistoric humps against the dry grass plains. "There would be a ceremony before the hunt, wouldn't there?" he asked.

"The briefest of ceremonies, sir."

"And after the hunt, the buffalo would have to be skinned and butchered."

"Our women are most adept, sir. It would be a matter of only the smallest part of an hour."

"And there is the other matter," Kincaid said.

"The other matter?"

"Your men, of course, have no weapons at all to hunt with. Or if they do," Matt reminded Dancing Horse, "our agreement has been broken. Therefore, since you are an honorable man, I assume there are no weapons available to hunt the buffalo."

"My men are wonderful improvisers, sir."

"I think only of their safety," Matt said with mock sincerity. "To be trapped among the herd, which will undoubtedly run, without a weapon—why, it is suicide. I am too great a friend of the Cheyenne to allow that, Dancing Horse."

Dancing Horse frowned and then smiled, nodding in surrender. "They would have enjoyed it."

"I don't doubt that. However, if your men . . . improvise weapons, then we have armed Cheyenne, armed soldiers, and armed Crow. I foresee certain possible complications in that situation, Dancing Horse."

"Yes," he sighed, looking at the buffalo from clear eyes that peered out of a wind-tanned, weather-lined face. "One last hunt," he said wistfully, "would have been a grand celebration. But, to be honest—and we must be—you have some logic on your side of the discussion, Lieutenant Kincaid."

"To be honest," Matt replied, "I think it would do my own heart good to watch your men ride among the buffalo and hunt, free and wild as they ever were. But my duty must overrule such impulses."

"Yes, duty," Dancing Horse said meditatively. "I well understand the constraints of duty, sir. By the way," he went on, changing the subject, "I did speak to the girl, Spring Walk, as you suggested. Her story, I am afraid, is more like the soldier's than like Two Fingers'."

"Good. I am happy to hear my man was not breaking the rules."

"Two Fingers was jealous. He wants the girl badly for his wife. She refuses him, although her father encourages it. He sees rivals everywhere."

"I have spoken to the soldier. There will be no more cause for jealousy."

"So I hope. Two Fingers is one of our more ingenious improvisers, sir."

With the faintest of smiles, Dancing Horse turned his pony aside and rode back toward the head of the column.

Corporal Wojensky drifted up to join his lieutenant.

"Everything quiet, sir?" Wojensky asked, nodding after the Cheyenne chief.

"Let's say that we are in a lull," Kincaid responded.

"Meaning you expect trouble, sir?" Wojensky inquired.

"Meaning, Corporal, that while we are here the possibility exists. We have women and we have men with guns. While we have that combination, I'm afraid the possibility does exist."

five ─────────────

She sat dejectedly on the edge of the unmade bed, her chin cradled in her hands, her eyes fixed on the fresh pile of dirt in the middle of what was otherwise a newly swept floor.

At the tap on the door, Pamela's eyes shifted, but she did not move. A second tap dragged her to her feet and she shuffled to the door, her hand pressed against her aching back.

She opened the door to Flora Conway, who stood there with a smile and an armful of wildflowers.

"I thought these might brighten the place up a little, dear," Flora said.

"I can plant them right over there," Pamela Drake said dryly.

Flora looked past her at the mound of earth on the floor. "It happens, but dear, dear, that's quite a mess."

"I just swept the floor."

"I know, it's awful, isn't it? No matter—we'll have it cleaned up in no time. I mind the time," Flora confided, "that a big chunk of wet sod fell right onto my table, smack into the cake I'd baked for the regimental chaplain."

Flora picked up the broom and began sweeping. "It's the way the roof is built. It's sod, you know, over planking. But some of the planking is just not very tight. When it rains . . . well, never mind when it rains, I don't think you'd want to hear about it."

"I honestly don't know how you can bear it," Pamela

said. She touched her hair nervously and watched as Flora picked up the dirt with a dustpan and walked to the door to throw it out.

"It's very difficult, dear," Flora said honestly. "The only thing that makes it tolerable, really, is having good friends and a man you truly love. Fortunately, you will have both of those."

"Yes." Pamela was silent and thoughtful as Flora continued her sweeping. "I was sure Sergeant Cohen said he would have someone come and fill the wood box for me," she said suddenly. "It was terribly cold last night."

"Didn't he send someone?" Flora asked. "That's not in the least like Sergeant Cohen. When he says something will be done, it's usually done."

"That's what I thought," Pamela said with some confusion. "But the wood box is still being used for something else. I don't know what you would call these."

She held up a buffalo chip daintily, and Flora smiled. She set the broom aside and walked to the girl. "Dear, dear Pamela, that is your fuel for the fire. There are so few trees out on the prairie that we use buffalo chips mostly."

"Buffalo chips?" She looked again at the flat, round object in her hand. "Does that mean what I think it does?"

"I'm afraid so."

"Ugh." Pamela dropped it back into the wood box and wiped her hand on her apron. She looked slowly around the room, with its worn furniture and leaky roof, as if it were a sort of betrayal. "I'm just not sure anymore," she murmured.

"Sit down." Flora stretched out a hand, and Pamela came to sit beside her on the bed. "You know you have a good man picked out. You know we all like you."

"Yes, but—"

"Sh." Flora placed a finger to Pamela's lips. She looked intently into the younger woman's eyes. "We do all welcome you. Tad Cambury is in love with you. But you know, dear, if you are not certain about this, about living out here, it's not too late to change your mind."

56

"It's not that. . . . Yes it is," she said dismally. A small clod of earth fell to the floor, and Pamela gazed at it helplessly.

"It's not only that, dear. You know, a woman can put up with anything if she truly loves a man. But sometimes a woman just gets the notion that she might like to marry as sort of an adventure."

"It's not like that," Pamela protested without much vigor.

"Oh, I didn't think so," Flora answered tactfully. "But sometimes, when it comes very close to being time, a woman thinks about other men." Here, Flora tried valiantly to pretend that she was speaking in generalities.

"Oh?" Pamela seemed to color slightly. "Did you?"

"I couldn't even *see* any other men, dear. That's when I knew that I would be happy with Warner Conway wherever we lived, under any conditions. And I'm sure you feel the same way about Tad Cambury." Flora stood and went on, "Otherwise, I know you're too clever a girl to enter a lifelong contract."

Pamela sat there, saying nothing. She was preoccupied now, and Flora hoped she was doing the right thing. Maybe the hint that she had been discovered would be enough to sway her one way or the other, either to marry Tad Cambury and be faithful, or decide right now that marriage and army life was not for her.

Flora added one last subtle hint. "Mrs. Cohen and I will be happy to schedule a day to help you really scrub and pretty up the place if you like, Pamela. I'll leave that up to you, if you decide that you do want some help."

Pamela turned those huge green eyes on Flora Conway. She said nothing, but there seemed to be something decisive going on behind those eyes. As if to help her along with her decision, another clod of earth fell from the roof.

Over their noon meal, Flora explained the entire incident to Warner Conway.

He frowned deeply and chided her lightly for meddling.

"But," he said, "I suppose it had to be done. And God

knows, I haven't got the grace to pull it off. You don't think she guessed that you knew?"

"I don't think so. I hope not. After all, Warner, she may decide to stay. She may marry Mister Cambury and make a devoted wife. It would be difficult to look her in the eye daily if she thought I knew, don't you think?"

"Yes, if she has any pride. It was just a lark, I suppose. A fling." He took a deep breath and let it out again, slowly. "I hope the girl makes the right decision—whatever that may be. I only wish it hadn't been Fairchild. Damn! This sort of recklessness is contrary to everything his father believes in."

"But he is not old John Fairchild, Warner."

"No, of course not." Warner rubbed his arm. His expression was concerned. "Yet I wouldn't do a thing in the world to hurt John Fairchild. I owe him a debt of friendship as well as my life. Still...I'll have to talk to young Mr. Fairchild. There was another incident, involving Sergeant Olsen."

"Sergeant Olsen!" Flora was astonished.

Warner nodded slowly. "Exactly. I can't recall anyone ever having trouble with Gus Olsen. His record is absolutely spotless." He rose heavily from his chair, leaving his napkin. "It appears I will have to have a talk with young Mr. Fairchild. A very serious talk."

The water at the Powder River crossing was icy and sweet. The horses drank while a few hardy Cheyenne splashed and played in the quick, cold current.

Farther along, there was a shallow oxbow where some of the women washed clothing, beating the garments against the large gray boulders.

Stretch Dobbs watched the women at their work. More exactly, he watched the tall, slender woman nearest him. She had long, glossy hair, and when she glanced up from her washing, she had a winning, bright smile for the tall soldier.

Wolfgang Holzer sauntered up to stand beside Dobbs.

"It is a fine morning," Holzer said. Dobbs blinked with mild surprise. That was a speech for Wolfie—it was seldom that he strung more than three English words together.

"A fine morning," Dobbs had to agree. The sunlight was streaming through the oaks along the riverbank. The silver river rolled away peacefully. A lone crow wheeled through the clear blue sky. "You know what makes it finer?" Dobbs said. That squaw there," he said nodding. "Tall for a Cheyenne woman, ain't she? Look there! She smiled again, see that?"

"Yes. It is a fine morning." Holzer nodded and wandered off to talk to one of the Contraries. It was bound to be an interesting conversation, Dobbs thought.

He glanced over his shoulder and then walked down nearer the river, watching the woman's quick, strong hands, her narrow hips, those deep, doe eyes.

"You are a good worker," Dobbs said.

She glanced up and smiled. Then she hid her giggle behind a modest hand.

"My name's Dobbs," he said, hunkering down. He plucked a few blades of grass and tossed them away. "What's your name, darlin'?"

She giggled again, and Dobbs smiled toothily. The woman glanced around and then told him, "Quail Feather."

"Quail Feather. That's a pretty name, ain't it? Nearly as pretty as you," he said, and the woman turned away, still giggling.

Dobbs saw a patch of blue among the oaks, moving toward him, and he rose, taking a few strides back. It was Kincaid, and Dobbs didn't care to be seen so close to the women. He contented himself with admiring the woman from afar. She hoisted her buckskin skirt once, and the sunlight flashed on her tapered brown calves, and Dobbs took a deep, dreamy breath.

Upriver a hundred yards, the cooking fires were going. Lone Pine sat with his friends, watching as his wife spooned stew into a wooden bowl. Flower crossed the clearing and gave her husband his meal.

The Crow scouts sat together in the shade of a sycamore nearer the river. They had opened tins of beef and peaches obtained from an army sutler. Now they smoked, Lone Pine noted with jealous irritation. He had not seen tobacco in half a year, and it looked like it would be a long while yet before he had any.

The youngest of the Crow scouts stuffed his clay pipe carelessly, not even bothering to pick up the tobacco that spilled onto his lap. He dusted it away carelessly and lit his pipe. His eyes were on the Cheyenne as he leaned back against the tree and puffed contentedly.

"Crow dog," Lone Pine muttered.

Two Fingers was beside him, and he egged Lone Pine on. "Plenty tobacco, plenty silver. The Crow are rewarded for cowardice."

"They will pay," Lone Pine boasted. Two Fingers shrugged in what Lone Pine took as a gesture of doubt. He scowled at the Crow and then came abruptly to his feet, dropping his bowl.

Flower was walking toward the trio of Crow scouts, and in her hands was a bowl of stew. She walked to the smoking man and stood before him. He glanced up finally, and Flower said, "I saw you did not eat much. Perhaps it is not good to eat from a can, with no woman's cooking to warm you."

"You are kind," the Crow said. "I, Badger Eyes, thank you."

Iron Owl started to say something, knowing that Badger Eyes was wading into trouble, but before he could speak, the shot rang out.

A bullet slammed into the trunk of the sycamore not ten inches from Badger Eyes' head. Scrambling to their feet, grabbing for their own weapons, they saw the smoke curling from an antiquated muzzle-loader in Lone Pine's hands.

Slowly, carefully, the Cheyenne reloaded the primitive weapon. Enraged, Badger Eyes charged across the space between them and drove his lowered shoulder into Lone Pine's chest. The two men toppled to the earth not two feet from the cooking fire, which still burned hotly.

Lone Pine clawed at the Crow's eyes with his hands and brought a knee up sharply, trying for Badger Eyes' groin. The Crow was quick, however. He rolled aside, got to his feet, and drove a moccasined foot into Lone Pine's ribs. He tried to kick his skull, but the Cheyenne got a grip on his ankle and flipped him backwards.

Matt Kincaid had come at a dead run, Rafferty and Malone at his heels. He broke into the camp in time to see Lone Pine dive at the Crow and be repelled by Badger Eyes' feet.

Lone Pine felt the wind rush from him, and he staggered before tripping and falling into the fire. He yowled with pain and lunged at the Crow, clawing him with his fingers as the Crow danced away, reaching for the knife that hung from his belt.

Matt shouldered his way through the crowd of cheering Cheyenne. One of their own was combating a hated Crow, and they chanted Lone Pine's name, and whistled and clapped.

Badger Eyes was crouched low now, his hair in his eyes. His silk shirt was torn down the back. The sunlight glittered on the knife blade.

He cut out at Lone Pine, and drew blood from a thin scratch across the Cheyenne's abdomen. Lone Pine screamed with rage and lunged for his rifle, which was unloaded, the ramrod still in the barrel. But he had no intention of firing it.

Lone Pine hefted the musket by the barrel; wielding it like an ax, he swung down viciously. The stock of the rifle slammed into Badger Eyes' shoulder, close to the neck, and the Crow went down in a heap.

Panting, grimacing exultantly, Lone Pine moved in, raising his rifle to strike again. Kincaid stepped behind him and grabbed the rifle, twisting it savagely away from the Cheyenne.

Lone Pine turned to Kincaid, his hands going for Matt's throat. Malone reached for his pistol and Rafferty moved

61

in, but none of it was necessary. A bronzed hand shot out and took Lone Pine by the shoulder, squeezing hard enough in the right place to drive the warrior to his knees.

"I apologize," Dancing Horse said. He still held Lone Pine on his knees. Badger Eyes, the Crow, struggled to his feet, and for a minute Matt thought the Crow would start it up again, but Iron Owl clamped his arms around his scout's chest, pinning his arms to his sides.

"We must speak," the Crow leader said, and Matt nodded. Dancing Horse slowly released Lone Pine, and the brave stood. He rubbed his shoulder and looked at his burned arm. Seeing his wife, he puffed out his chest triumphantly, but Flower simply spun on her heel and walked away.

"Come, brother," Two Fingers said, putting an arm around Lone Pine. The two brooding Cheyenne walked away together, casting a last defiant glance at Matt Kincaid.

Matt picked up his hat, which had fallen, dusted it, and nodded his head. Dancing Horse and Iron Owl followed him to a gray, barren oak that stood at the river's edge.

Dancing Horse spoke first, with controlled anger. "The Crow must be punished."

"I can hardly punish a man for getting angry after he was shot at," Matt responded. "Especially since Badger Eyes got the worst of the scuffle. His collar bone might be broken."

Dancing Horse seemed to enjoy that fact. Iron Owl was scowling heavily, liking none of it.

"To speak of punishment is a mockery!" the Crow leader said. "We sat apart, as we were told to do. We ate our meal. A shameless Cheyenne squaw flirted with Badger Eyes, and her husband shot at him. Now who should be punished, old Cheyenne?"

Iron Owl emphasized "old" heavily, and Dancing Horse's eyes went cold. Matt stepped in immediately, reminding them who was in charge.

"There will be no punishment." At Iron Owl's objection, Matt held up a hand. "Lone Pine deserves it. He deserves to walk in hobbles to the Nation. But he is a man who has been humiliated. I hardly think we will solve the problem by adding to that humiliation.

"But," Matt went on, "there will be no forgiveness next time. I want you to make that clear to him, Dancing Horse. Nor will I tolerate reprisals, Iron Owl. This is finished as of now. Is that understood?"

"It is," Iron Owl said. He stared at Dancing Horse from behind heavily hooded eyes. The veins in his throat pulsed, standing out against the hard muscle there.

Dancing Horse simply ignored the Crow until Iron Owl finally turned and stalked away to see to his injured man. When the Crow was gone, Matt said, "There was a weapon, Dancing Horse. Improvised?"

"I cannot say." Dancing Horse's manner was entirely different now. Brittle, taciturn, he seemed to feel that Kincaid was siding with the Crow against his tribe.

"I want all those weapons turned over to me now."

The Cheyenne shrugged. "Who knows if there are more?"

"I do, damn it!" Kincaid was stirred up now. "You knew they had weapons and I knew it. I didn't search for them because I know you've got people who feel that they aren't warriors, aren't men without their rifles, their bows. I didn't want them to feel deprived, but now, damn it, they're on the verge of depriving other men—of their lives. And next time it could damn well be a soldier. I want those weapons, Dancing Horse, and I want them now."

He made it even clearer. "If they're not forthcoming, voluntarily, now, I'll search until I find them. We're not moving until I see a stack of bows, rifles, knives, and arrows out there in that clearing. I'll not destroy anything. I'll turn them over to the agent at Darlington. But I want them all under my guard. Do you understand?"

"Yes." Dancing Horse muttered the word. He was looking into the far distance, his arms crossed. Matt guessed that he was undercutting Dancing Horse's power by doing this. The chief had smiled at the order from the Indian agent, winked as the men hid their favorite buffalo guns, and that

63

had gained him respect. Well, he thought, to hell with Dancing Horse's feelings. There was no need for anyone to die on this journey, not from hunger, cold, exertion, or gunshot.

And if things continued the way they were going, someone—Crow, Cheyenne or soldier—was sure as hell going to be killed.

"I will ask," Dancing Horse said casually. "Maybe someone has another weapon; I would not know."

"Please do," Matt said. At that, Dancing Horse turned and strode back toward the Cheyenne, who stood in a cluster now, watching his approach.

Wojensky was standing by with Rafferty, Dobbs, and Malone. "Don't let anyone slip out of camp in the next hour, Wojensky."

"No, sir."

The soldiers spread out, encircling the camp. The Cheyenne, obviously growing indignant if not outright hostile as Dancing Horse spoke, grumbled and raised occasional shouts. Matt Kincaid sat his horse, watching them until Dancing Horse made a final exhoration and the warriors dispersed, going to their packs.

The first warrior to return to the clearing was Lone Pine. He flung his bow and quiver down, and threw his knife so that it struck point first and imbedded itself in the loamy soil.

That defiant but harmless act brought a cheer of approval from the others, and after that, each weapon that appeared from out of a blanket roll or tipi was hurled to the ground.

Matt walked his horse to where the Crow scouts sat tending Badger Eyes' wounded shoulder.

"Is he all right?"

"Yes." Iron Owl was stone-faced.

Matt thought it was best to leave them alone, and so he turned his horse away after first telling them, "I have punished the Cheyenne. You see now they have no weapons."

Iron Owl stood from his bandaging and said; "They were supposed to have none before, Lieutenant Kincaid."

There was nothing to say to that thinly veiled intimation that Kincaid had not done his job, and so he turned his eyes toward the camp once more.

"Looks like that's all of them, sir," Wojensky said. "Only way to be sure is to search their belongings article by article."

"No, we'll save them that indignity, Wojensky. They're hostile enough, and it's a long road yet. Only two days gone—Jesus, I'm beginning to wonder if we're going to make it to Oklahoma."

"We'll make it, sir. Trouble is, you're too tolerant."

"Maybe," Matt agreed quietly. But, he thought, what was he to do? These were a beaten people being transported against their will. They didn't need a slavemaster. He silently cursed the bureaucrat who had assigned the Crow scouts in the first place. Then he looked to the peaceful peaks of the Bighorn Mountains. Placid, unconcerned, timeless, they stood in solitude against a pale sky.

"Get those weapons gathered up," Kincaid said abruptly. "We've got half a day's traveling time left."

John Fairchild, Jr. slammed the door to the BOQ, and Fitzgerald glanced up from his hand. Taylor had just wagered a nickel on three fours, and Fitz, who had eights and sevens, had been ready to be suckered in. Now he folded and turned in his chair to face the sullen Fairchild.

"I'm Fitzgerald," he said by way of introduction.

Fairchild only nodded, sitting on the edge of his bunk. "I can't believe it," he said with disgust. "The CO just chewed my butt. He took sides with an enlisted man!" Fairchild's expression was one of total disbelief.

Fitz glanced at Taylor, who was stacking his nickels and dimes. Taylor shook his head imperceptibly.

"It happens," Fitzgerald said consolingly.

Taylor riffled the cards and dealt again. Fitz picked up his hand, fanned it, and arranged the pair of jacks to one side, the trash cards to the other. Fairchild wandered over, unbuttoning his tunic.

"A fucking enlisted man," he said bitterly. Eliciting no further sympathy, he shrugged. "Conway's supposed to be a friend of my old man, too. My old man saved his fucking life!"

"Three cards," Fitz said, tossing the trash cards away. He drew nothing and tried to conceal the fact from Taylor. But Taylor had a notion and threw in fifteen cents. Fitzgerald threw his hand in immediately. He stretched and yawned again.

"Mind if I sit in?" Fairchild asked. Fitz glanced up at him, shrugged, and nodded to a chair. "If you want. Two-handed's not much good. I've got to warn you, though, there's only fifty-one cards in this deck. Three of hearts is missing."

"No problem." Fairchild winked and walked to his locker, returning with a crisp new deck. "I travel prepared," he said, reversing his chair.

Taylor took the new deck and shuffled. Fairchild was digging in his pockets for change, complaining as he did so. "Hell of a fine friend Conway is, huh? A goddamned enlisted man, and he sticks up for him."

"Everyone gets chewed out sometimes," Fitzgerald said, cutting the deck. "It'll pass."

"A fucking enlisted man," Fairchild said, shaking his head as he picked up the cards. "If that bastard Conway—"

"Look," Taylor said sharply, "I don't intend to discuss Captain Conway here, not in this manner."

"Sure, sure, I understand," Fairchild said confidentially. It was clear, however, that he had no idea at all that he was alone in his criticism. "It's only that—"

"Nickel ante, any pair opens," Fitzgerald said, cutting the new complaint off.

They played a desultory hand, and then another. Fairchild went on with his babbling, but it didn't affect his game. He won two of the next three hands.

Fitzgerald knew it wasn't his night. He was dealt two

66

fours, a six, a nine, and a trey. He discarded the three trash cards and got a seven, another six, and a queen to replace them. Nevertheless, he opened.

Fairchild raised a dime and Taylor stuck with him, but Fitz folded, stretching his arms overhead. The door to the BOQ opened and he glanced that way.

He stood there as dismal and as whipped as any man Fitzgerald had ever seen. Fitz got to his feet. "What the hell is it, Tad?"

Cambury shook his head and walked toward his bed as if he were made of stone. There were tears in his eyes, Fitzgerald now saw, and he walked that way, leaving Taylor and Fairchild to their strategy.

Cambury looked up at Fitzgerald with blank eyes. His hands were trembling.

"What in God's name happened, Tad?"

"She's leaving, Fitz. Tomorrow."

"Leaving? Pamela?"

"She's leaving me," he repeated. "Changed her mind about getting married." He shrugged helplessly.

"Why?"

"She didn't say why, Fitz. Honest to God, I don't understand it. I just don't."

"Have you talked to her about it, tried to find out if there was something—"

"That's where I've been. I've talked and pleaded until . . . Christ." He threw up his hands. "She's going, and that's it." Cambury leaned back on his pillow, staring at the ceiling.

Taylor was looking at Fitzgerald from across the room. Taylor did know something about it, even if Cambury didn't, Fitzgerald was sure.

"Aces and tens," Taylor said.

"Three fours, Lieutenant," Fairchild said, and raked in the pile of coins. "Another hand?"

"That's it for me," Taylor said.

"How about a beer, then? At the sutler's."

"No." Taylor shook his head. "That's enough excitement for me. Besides, we're riding night patrol. It doesn't mix with alcohol."

"It's three-point-two, for God's sake," Fairchild laughed. "A man can't get decently high."

"He doesn't know Private Malone, obviously," Fitzgerald commented.

"How about you, Fitzgerald? You're not going on duty?"

"No, thanks," Fitz said.

Fairchild didn't bother to ask Cambury. If he had as much as noticed Tad lying there, he gave no indication of it. He simply pocketed his winnings, swept the cards from the table, and walked out, still buttoning his tunic.

Taylor stood wearily and walked to where Fitzgerald stood watching the closed door. "How about some air?" Taylor said, and Fitzgerald nodded.

Taylor got both of their hats and they stepped out, walking toward the mess hall a ways before stopping on the boardwalk.

"What is it, then?" Fitz wanted to know.

"You read me that good? You should win at poker more often."

"I know something's eating at you. Is it Cambury or Fairchild?"

"Both," Taylor answered, and in response to Fitz's curious expression, he told him all about it. When he was finished, Fitz was silent for a long minute, staring up at the cold stars.

"The son of a bitch," he said softly.

"Yeah," Taylor said cynically. "He's a jewel, isn't he?"

"Say," Fitzgerald said abruptly, as if changing the subject, "what did Fairchild take that last pot with?"

Taylor frowned. "Three fours, why?"

"Then I'll tell you something else about Mr. Fairchild. He cheats at cards—I folded a pair of fours."

six ————————————

They camped that evening on twin grassy knolls a mile outside of Gillette, Wyoming. The Cheyenne were unusually silent, and Kincaid did not like it. Dancing Horse had advised Kincaid that they were short on beef already, although Matt did not think it was possible. It was more likely that Dancing Horse had decided to make the trip no more enjoyable for Kincaid than it was for the Cheyenne. To that end, he had begun complaining about this and that— the length of the day's trek, the cold of the night, insufficient time for breaking and setting up camp, and now the supposed lack of beef.

"This is cattle country," Matt told Wojensky after confiding in him. "Let's see if we can pick up a dozen head or so."

"Ride into Gillette?"

"I think so. Cut out Malone, if you can find him. You two ride in with me. If we can find any beef in town, I'll give you the chance to practice your cowboying."

That had become a running joke, but a black one since the night Kip Schoendienst had gotton a snootful and ridden off toward Texas.

Wojensky rose, wiping his hands on his pants. It was nearly dark, and from the knoll they could see the lights of Gillette. Matt told Wojensky, "Leave Rafferty in charge, and advise the Crow scouts. The Cheyenne are bedding down, so there shouldn't be any trouble. But I don't want any of our Indians going any nearer to town."

Wojensky nodded and saluted. Kincaid didn't have to go into a lengthy explanation. There had been a massacre near Gillette not two years ago. Whether any of Dancing Horse's band had participated or not, Matt could not say. But they were Cheyenne and there was bound to be some lingering animosity.

It was full dark before Malone and Wojensky reported back, and by the time the three soldiers trailed into Gillette, the stores were dark and shuttered, the saloons ablaze with light.

Kincaid stopped first by the jailhouse, a brick building set apart from the rest of the town, but the place was locked and dark.

"Looks like the law keeps banker's hours," Wojensky commented. "Where to, sir?"

"The first saloon," Matt answered. The saloons seemed to be the only establishments open, and it was there that the locals hung out, exchanging information. If there was beef to be had, someone in the saloon would likely know of it. Malone had a hungry look on his face, Kincaid noticed as they passed through the glare of a lamp hanging in front of the stable on Main Street.

"This is business, Private Malone."

"Oh, I know it, sir," Malone said. Kincaid was hardly reassured. Malone's reputation as a drinker—a bad drinker—was firmly entrenched.

"Have two if you want, no more," Matt said, softening a little. It was a long trail for Malone as well.

"Yes, sir!" Malone chirped, straightening up a bit. By God, he had always said that Matt Kincaid was a good officer.

They swung down and hitched their horses to the already crowded tie rail in front of the saloon, which the faded sign identified as Trail's End.

The saloon itself was long and narrow, with a rough plank bar along the eastern wall, and two long puncheon tables opposite. A warped roulette wheel stood unused in the far corner. The room was heavy with smoke and loud chatter.

The talking quieted momentarily as the three soldiers entered, and then resumed. Kincaid eased up to the bar, with Malone and Wojensky beside him. The bartender glanced up, but it was a minute before he moved over to them.

Kincaid took the time to glance at the pictures of women, horses, and dogs, cut out of magazines, which had been pinned to the walls, and to study the occasional hostile or, more often, merely curious faces of the roughly dressed men in the saloon.

"What'll you have?" the bartender asked. He was burly and balding, with a surprisingly high-pitched voice.

"Beer," Kincaid said. Wojensky nodded agreement. Malone opted for whiskey.

In response to Kincaid's critical glance, Malone said, "If I'm only havin' two, I want to know I've had something."

When the bartender returned, carrying two mugs in one hand, the foam slopping over and running down his sleeve, Malone's whiskey in the other, Kincaid asked him about beef.

"I can't say," the bartender replied, rubbing his stubbled jaw. "Of course, there's plenty of stock on the big ranches outside of town, but you need it tonight?" Kincaid nodded. "I can't say. Rafe!"

At the sound of his name, Rafe swiveled toward them. A man of fifty, weathered and grizzled, he wore worn range clothes and a drooping, tobacco-stained mustache. The bartender waved him over.

"He's the foreman of the Rafter H," the barman explained as Rafe approached. "He'll know what's around close."

"This here's Lieutenant Kincaid," the bartender said. "Rafe Marsh."

Marsh stuck out his hand cautiously, and they shook. Malone was already on his second whiskey, not wanting

71

to miss out if Kincaid decided abruptly to leave. "What can I do fer ya?"

Kincaid explained briefly that he needed a dozen head of beef tonight, or in the morning at the latest.

"That's tough. There might be a few culls in the holding pens. The buyer turned thumbs-down on some Slash J cows, and Johnson didn't want to drive 'em home. Usually they disappear—I figure they show up on the restaurant platters within the next few days. Sometimes the Arapaho slip in and make off with 'em. Prime beef?" He shook his head. "No. Nobody's holding anything near enough to do you any good. Except maybe..." he turned around, cupped his brown hands to his mouth, and shouted above the din.

"Barney! Just hold on a minute, Lieutenant. Hey, Barney, come here!"

A tall man with dark, hooded eyes and a whiskey swagger to his gait moved toward them. He stared sullenly at Kincaid. "Man wants some beef tonight—dawn at the latest," Rafe said.

"Why talk to me?" Barney asked.

"Come on, Barney, everyone knows you got some cows—kind of a mixed herd—stuck away somewheres near."

"Maybe," Barney said, glancing around casually.

The bartender had started to whisk away Malone's glass, but Malone shook his head, pantomiming another round. Wojensky caught it out of the corner of his eye, but kept silent rather than interrupt the lieutenant in his negotiations.

"I've got a few, maybe," Barney said. "What would this be. Army voucher?"

"Cash money," Kincaid told him.

Barney's eyebrows lifted with interest. "Yeah, how many head we talking about?"

"Only a dozen," Matt told him. He saw Malone down his drink, and was surprised that it had lasted him so long. He returned his gaze, to the dark, lean face of Barney. Jake hadn't said so outright, but Matt had the impression that Barney was a rustler. Perhaps that was too strong a term;

mavericks on the range belonged to whoever slapped a brand on them first. Strictly speaking, it was illegal and discouraged violently by the big ranchers, but unless caught in the act, it was difficult to prove. Besides, many of those who were now big ranchers had gotten their start in the same way.

"We can deal," Barney said finally. "I'll take ten dollars a head."

"You'll take eight," Kincaid said.

"I'll take eight," Barney said after a moment. "Mind if I ask why you're buyin'? Don't the army supply you men with beef anymore?"

"It's for some Cheyenne," Matt said. "We're escorting them down to the Indian Nation."

"Cheyenne?" Barney asked mildly. Matt noticed that the man was gripping the edge of the bar tightly.

"Yes."

"Then go to hell. I don't need money that bad. I'll not feed the savages. Let 'em drink blood."

"Now wait a minute."

"*You* wait! Cheyenne killed my wife, killed my brother, killed my son. Six years old he was. They killed 'em for nothin'. For sport!" Barney was hardly in control of himself now. Heads turned toward them as the cattleman's voice rose tremulously. "Let 'em drink blood like they always have—or let 'em die. Do the world a favor."

"I do sympathize," Matt told him with sincerity. "As a soldier, I have also lost friends to the Cheyenne. But these poeple are not fighting men any longer. As I've said, they're being transported to the Indian Nation."

"Do me a favor—transport 'em to hell," Barney said with a dirty wink.

There was nothing further to say. Matt had lost the bargain, that was obvious, and there was no point in arguing the Indian problem with this half-drunk, belligerent cowhand.

"I'm sorry we couldn't do business," Matt said. "Good evening."

Matt turned his back to Barney, and Jake, shrugging, moved away. But Barney was not through. Whether it was the liquor, his righteous indignation, or the boost of having all eyes on him, he kept it up.

"An army man sticking up for them butchers is disgusting. What the hell kind of soldier are you? You fought 'em and you baby 'em anyway! I'll bet you fought 'em. Fought 'em from a damned desk."

"Corporal," Matt said to Wojensky, "it's time we were riding."

"Don't ignore me," Barney said truculently. "You turn your back on me and then you ignore me."

"I see nothing else to be done—but to ignore you, sir."

Barney put his hand on Matt's shoulder, and Matt flicked it away. "I don't like you, bluejacket."

"The liquor's getting you off on the wrong track," Kincaid replied. "If you don't like Indians—go find a Cheyenne to argue with. I don't intend to stand here and debate."

"Debatin's not what I've got in mind."

Matt again turned his back and paid the bartender. Malone downed a last surreptitious drink and tugged his hat down. Barney was so close to Kincaid that his breath, rank and whiskey-sour, sprayed the lieutenant's face.

"I just plain don't like you, *Lieutenant*," Barney said, "and I'm damned if you're leaving this bar until I've got my satisfaction."

"I have no intention of brawling with you, sir," Kincaid said.

"You got no choice, boy!"

Barney once again took hold of Kincaid's tunic, his eyes bulging. It was all too much for Malone, who was warm with whiskey. This was his environment—a smoky bar, a rowdy drunk. He simply handled it as he usually did.

Barney lifted a menacing fist and Malone stepped in and hammered a perfect right hook to the shelf of the cattleman's jaw. Barney's eyes rolled back and he dropped to his knees, balancing there a moment before he toppled over, his head buoncing off the wooden floor of the saloon.

Kincaid turned to Wojensky and said crisply, "Corporal, this soldier is drunk. Place him under arrest."

"Yes, sir," Wojensky said.

Others in the saloon had started to rise, sensing a brawl, but this move by Kincaid put the lid on it. He turned to the roomful of men.

"I apologize for this soldier's disgraceful behavior. He shall be punished."

Already, Wojensky had propelled Malone to the door and out into the street. Kincaid nodded and followed them.

Outside, Malone and Wojensky were mounted, and Matt stepped into the saddle without hesitation. "Let's ride," he suggested.

A few hardcases, drinks in hand, had filtered out onto the boardwalk, and Matt turned his horse, leading the others quickly past the city limits.

Malone wobbled slightly in his saddle, and Kincaid smiled. "It *was* getting a little tiresome, wasn't it?"

"Most tiresome, sir. And it ain't right for an officer to have to grovel with trash like that—but I don't mind takin' 'em on. Reg'lar business, you might say."

"I'll have to reprimand you, you know."

"I did consider that first, sir," Malone answered. His speech was thick, and Matt grinned.

"Never did see a man get soused on two drinks."

"They were stiff, sir. Mighty stiff."

"Well," Kincaid admitted, "I suppose it was my fault— I didn't have to say anything about the beef being for the Cheyenne. I won't repeat that mistake."

Malone's horse had drifted away from them, and Malone himself seemed to be off in a fog, unconcerned with the direction of his mount.

"He does have his useful points, sir," Wojensky said.

"It appears so."

"If there's a fight, he's the man the boys want around them. Of course," he added honestly, "most of the time it's Malone who starts them."

The camp was silent when they reached it. The Crow

had a low fire glowing, burning itself to embers, but the Cheyenne, without exception it seemed, were asleep in their tipis.

Rafferty rode up to report no trouble, and they told him briefly what had happened. Malone dismounted, unsaddled, picketed his horse, and wobbled away. It was no novel sight, and Rafferty didn't comment about it.

After ordering the guard change, Matt Kincaid entered his tent, washed his torso with cool water, and sagged onto his cot. He was tired; his eyes felt as if they were filled with grit. He tried to sleep, but sleep did not come. He was worried.

The worrying took no definite form—it was simply an instinctive, nagging notion that disaster was hovering over the expedition, awaiting only the slightest whim of Fate to come crashing down on it, enveloping them all in bloody tragedy.

Malone staggered to his tent. He was alone there for the time being; Holzer was out on night guard. He plopped down on his cot and stared at the dark roof of the tent, not even covering himself with a blanket. The tent pole circled him dizzily, and when he closed his eyes, his cot inverted and the world spun away into a dark funnel.

He tried sleeping on his side, but it was no better. The whiskey had gotten to him again, not for the first time, nor the fiftieth. Malone sat up, putting his feet to the ground. He threw back his head, took six deep breaths, and nearly threw up.

Rising unsteadily, he wobbled to the flap of the tent and went out into the clear, cold night. The stars were diamonds spattered against a velvet sky. The river was mottled silver and black beneath a crescent moon.

Malone turned toward it, caught a toe on a rock, and went down on a shoulder. Cursing, he got to his feet and lurched on.

He got to his knees on the riverbank, and stripped off his shirt and washed his face, his shoulders, his chest with the icy water.

He threw back his head, shaking the water from his hair

like a dog. Then, shivering, partly sobered, he reached for his shirt. She handed it to him.

It was a moment before Malone's mind registered the unexpected apparition, and in that moment Spring Walk stepped against him and her parted lips met his. Some vague impulse told him to push her away, but he managed to pulverize that thought and brush it aside.

His arms went around her and he kissed her deeply. Her hands swept across his bare, damp back. "You better watch out, woman," Malone said, "you come around asking for trouble."

With her arms around his waist, she smiled up at him. The moonlight was in her eyes. "But I know you will do nothing to violate your leader's order." There was a teasing inflection to that, which Malone understood well enough.

"There's certain things it's just not possible to order a man not to do."

"Is that so?" she asked lightly. She cocked her head curiously, like a child questioning some deep mystery, but her hands were not those of a child. She cupped Malone's groin, feeling the swelling bulge there, letting her lips run across his chest.

"Come on," Malone said. The blood was pulsing in his head. They stood out in the open now, in the moonlight. He grabbed her wrist and led her into the willow brush along the river.

"Don't go away," Malone said. His fingers trembled as he sat down, leaning against the trunk of a sycamore to remove his boots.

He saw Spring Walk step from her buckskin dress, saw the moonlight gloss her body, highlighting breasts, firm thighs, softly curved buttocks, and he muttered to himself:

"Oh Gawd..." He fought with his boots, but Spring Walk, smiling, crouched down and pulled them off.

Malone unbuttoned his pants and Spring Walk took hold of the cuffs, slipping them free. Malone glanced around and saw no one, heard nothing—although he doubted right now that it would matter much.

His sex throbbed against his thigh. The cold night air did

nothing to discourage its ambitious swelling. Spring Walk stood over him, her legs spread, and his trembling hands ran up her thighs, which were incredibly smooth, silky over firm muscle. His fingers reached her crotch and probed her secret trove. Spring Walk crouched down slightly, spreading herself, her eyes closed, head thrown back. She murmured appreciatively as Malone explored her damp, soft depths.

Her legs, Malone noticed, had begun quivering, and now she opened her eyes, fixing them on him, and slowly settled against Malone, who still sat propped up against the base of the sycamore.

She sat facing him, her breasts grazing his pounding chest as she snuggled against him. Her crotch, so warm that Malone could feel her heat against his groin, was only inches over him, and he spread her with gentle fingers, drawing back the tiny curtains of flesh.

Spring Walk had her hands on his shoulders, and she lifted herself slightly as Malone took hold of his member and slipped it inside her.

"Don't wait for nothin' now, baby," Malone whispered, and she settled onto him, enveloping him, her breasts pressed against his chest, her tongue probing his mouth as her hands clenched his hard shoulders.

She swayed and rolled and jerked against him, and Malone felt himself going dizzy. The liquor might have had something to do with it, but the rest was the woman—flesh and hungry muscle moving against him, devouring him, her mouth whispering words he could not understand. . . .

He reached behind her a grasped her buttocks, thrusting himself against her as he squeezed so hard it must have hurt, but she said nothing, seemed not to notice as she followed her own demanding instincts.

Her voice was soft, her breasts soft against him; her scent was ripe, fragrant in his nostrils; her pelvis pounded against him.

She grew more savage. Her hips writhed and her hands tore at his flesh. Her teeth found his neck and she bit down hard. All of it only spurred Malone on toward a climax he could not deny, slow, or ignore. It was time, and he wanted to fill this woman, to split her, to impale her, and he jerked against her, his lips going from nipple to nipple, his hands gripping her shuddering ass.

Abruptly he came, and his legs pulsed with it, his abdomen rose and fell, the blood seemed to drain out of his head, his heart faltered.

He was through, but she was not. She thumped against him, spread her juices against him, hammered at his chest with her fists while her teeth tore at his ears, his throat, even his nose.

She writhed and swiveled, rose and plunged against him, and he held on for dear life. It was like being attacked, and he was. Savagely, sensuously attacked by a woman who wanted to express every fragment of her physical need.

He held her, and it was like wrestling a naked, overpoweringly strong woman. She struggled nearly as if she were trying to escape. Precisely like that—except for the slip and slosh of her crotch against him, the constant assault that brought him to the pulsing brink of a second climax.

He felt her go tense, felt himself emptying into her with a throbbing release, felt her tighten and draw against him.

And then, by God, she screamed at the top of her lungs!

It was a savage, raw, triumphant bugling. She had fought for, worked for, a physical treasure that she had found. And it had been every bit as rich, as golden as she had wanted.

She screamed out in savage joy, and Malone felt the muscles inside her go slack, felt her flood him, felt her collapse.

"Jesus Christ!" Malone was wriggling beneath her, and she responded with a delicious slow thrust of her hips.

"No . . ." Malone panted. "I have to get up. My God, that scream."

She still clung to him, working her pelvis against his, and he knew in a panicked insight that she did not care if they were discovered, cared for nothing but the moment. She draped herself around his neck, her breasts pressed to him, her fluid hips working steadily as Malone's panic increased.

"I have to go." He took her arms from around his neck,

and she looked at him with disappointment. Her eyes were deep with moonlight and emotion. She kissed his chest, let her fingers run across his legs, but Malone still had that scream echoing in his ears.

Someone was coming through the brush, or he thought so. He could see it now: discovered by Cheyenne warriors, raping a woman in the brush. *God.* He shoved her away, felt his wilting member fall free, and gathered up his clothes.

She sat there sadly and he stopped, came back, kissed her mouth twice, and was gone, trampling through the brush, his heart racing.

He ran upriver for five minutes and then stopped deep in a willow-and-cattail ticket, dressing hurriedly. He stamped into his boots and got to a cautious crouch, peering back downstream, expecting to see torchlight, a search party, Lieutenant Kincaid with a pistol in his hand and hell-to-pay on his face.

Nothing. There was nothing, and Malone slowly got to his feet. His heart still hammered, and sweat trickled down his shirt front.

Well, I'm damn sure sober anyway, he thought. Slowly then, he circled wide of the camp, coming up on the eastern perimeter. The camp slept; only the night guards wandered through the empty darkness. A nighthawk swooped low and screeched, and Malone nearly came apart.

Waving a fist at the darting bird, he made for the camp, circled it swiftly, and entered his dark, silent tent, where he lay down, drew a blanket up, and waited for his heart to still.

It took some time. Fifteen minutes, perhaps. Then his pulse slowed to a normal rate as the camp remained silent, and Malone stretched out, a slow smile spreading across his mouth to remain there as he slept peacefully, deeply through the night.

Stretch Dobbs slowly lifted his head. The moon was sinking low and there was a thin, haunting ground fog across the plains. He looked right and then left, seeing no one.

Minutes before, Malone had come tearing through the willows like he had hostiles on his tail. Stretch had ducked low, but nothing had happened, no one else had appeared. Maybe, he thought, Malone had seen some of those little blue snakes, like he had that other time.

He pushed Malone out of his mind.

There was room for only one thought there tonight. But would she come? Could she? He lifted his head, searching the night. She was not there, and Stretch began to despair.

Quail Feather. The name seemed soft and mysterious and promised much. Stretch lay back, his head on his clasped hands. He closed his eyes and smiled dreamily, thinking of how it would be . . . and then he did not have to imagine anymore.

He heard the rustling of the brush, the whisper of moccasined feet against the leaves underfoot, and then she was there, the moonlight shining on her pretty face.

"I am here, Stretch Dobbs," Quail Feather said softly.

She got down beside him, and Stretch put his hand behind her neck, drawing her mouth to his. She was a practiced, deft lover. Her kiss was tremulous, full of possibility. Her lips fluttered across his, drawing his mouth to hers.

He pulled her gently to him and kissed her again, his hand finding the swell of her hip where it rested easily.

"You are a long, lonesome man," she whispered. "Do you need me, Stretch Dobbs?"

"Yes," Stretch admitted heroically. She was close against him, her legs against his, and Stretch let his hand drop to the hem of her skirt.

He slipped it up inside, and Quail Feather purred into his ear. The night was chill and damp in the willows, but Stretch minded none of it. He kissed her again and let his hand run across her soft thigh.

"Yes, Stretch Dobbs, be my man," Quail Feather murmured.

His hand crept to her crotch and then stopped. There was something there that didn't belong. Long, hard. . . . He sat bolt upright, gazing at his hand as if it had been burned.

Dobb's eyes were as wide as twin Kansas moons. He sputtered, "You're a man!" He repeated it twice more, shaking the disbelief from his head.

"So?" Quail Feather got halfway up, resting his head on his hand. He smiled at Dobbs. "Are you not still a long, lonesome man?"

"God! A man!" Dobbs muttered. He looked around guiltily. "You son of a bitch," Dobbs said with slow disgust.

Quail Feather pouted. "Does that mean you no longer love your Quail Feather?"

"Love you! I ought to smash your face for you."

At that, Quail Feather burst into tears. He buried his face in his hands, and his shoulders rolled with his sobbing.

"Jesus," Dobbs muttered. He got to his feet. "Jesus Christ."

Then he turned away quickly, breaking his way angrily through the thicket, the sounds of Quail Feather's crying reaching after him through the night.

seven _____

Rafferty yawned as he came up to the morning fire. He crouched down, poured himself a cup of coffee from the granitewear pot, and nodded to Malone, who was beaming, Holzer, who looked merely pleasant, and Stretch Dobbs, who looked as if he had spent the night digging his own grave.

"Mornin', boys," Rafferty said. Getting no response but a nod from Holzer, he settled down in the shade of the oak to drink his coffee.

The camp below was beginning to stir. The tipis were already coming down, being carefully rolled as the campfires were started.

"Damnedest thing," Rafferty said, as if from out of the blue. "I got to talking with Wojensky last night. What happened was, we were on night guard and we seen this squaw slip out of the camp."

At that, both Malone and Dobbs lifted their heads sharply. Rafferty sipped his coffee and stretched.

"So?" Malone prodded.

"Well, we watched her come out and head into the bushes. So Wojensky says maybe we ought to drift down and turn her back. The lieutenant don't want any night prowlers."

Rafferty was silent for a minute. Malone leaned forward impatiently. "So?"

"So we drifted on down and we come upon her. It was

nothing, you see. She just come out to take care of private business."

"Oh," Dobbs said with relief.

"And that's the story?" Malone snapped.

"Give me a minute, Malone, would ya?" Rafferty leaned back on an elbow. "So we started to turn back when it hit me and Wo at the same time. Here was a woman, standing up against a tree, taking a leak."

Dobbs felt his heart sink. He looked away toward the Indian camp.

"It's a different culture," Malone said laconically.

"It sure as hell is, Malone. Wojensky and me we could just hardly keep from busting out laughing. Here comes this pretty little squaw, out she flips a big old pecker, and leans up against a tree to take a leak." Rafferty laughed in recollection. "Gawd—I tell you, that fried me.

"Later, Wojensky told me how it is. There's men among the Cheyenne who dress up like squaws, *become* squaws, as far as that goes. Living with the women, dressing like 'em, doing their chores. And everyone just goes along with it. The women just accept them as sisters."

"A frightening thought," Malone said with a smile. "Damn—can you imagine some poor son of a bitch trying to make one of 'em?"

Dobbs felt his ears go crimson. He forced himself to say casually, "Well, that's good enough reason to stay in bounds and not fool with *any* of the Cheyenne women, ain't it?"

"Now, Stretch," Malone drawled confidentially, "I wouldn't worry about that. There's plenty of real women down there. Hell, the odds are on your side."

Again, Dobbs flushed hotly. He was sure they knew about it, somehow knew. He started to say something when Rafferty shouted out, "Attention!"

"At ease," Kincaid said immediately.

The lieutenant crouched down by the fire and helped himself to a cup of coffee. "Good morning, men."

"Mornin', Lieutenant Kincaid." Malone answered.

"I'm glad to find you here, Malone," Kincaid said, and

Malone cursed silently, sure that he was about to be chewed out either for hitting the town man or. . . . She had screamed awfully loud—had he been seen with Spring Walk after all?

"You wanted something, sir?" Malone asked casually.

"Yes I did," Kincaid smiled. "I want you to do something for me, Malone. I want you to get into another fight."

Malone did a sharp double take, then tilted his head as if he had not heard correctly. "Sir?"

"I want you to fight someone for me, Malone," Matt said, sipping his coffee. "Tell me, have you ever lost intentionally?"

"Sir, I ain't no *professional!*" Malone said with injured dignity.

"Well, that's what I want you to do," Kincaid said. "I want you to fight. I want you to lose."

Malone and Rafferty exchanged a glance. Was Kincaid planning on betting some money, then?

"Who would it be, sir?" Malone asked warily.

"Two Fingers."

"Two Fingers!" Malone's brow furrowed. "I thought—"

"That I didn't want any trouble with the Cheyenne that could be avoided, you're right," Kincaid said. "But," he went on, "we have a tense situation here. The Cheyenne have had their pride stung. Their manhood is in question— at least they think so. Their women are flirting with the Crow . . . and with you men," Kincaid said in a way that made Malone wonder what he did know.

"So what's the fight got to do with it, sir?"

"Simple. I'd like to stage a sporting fight. You and a Cheyenne. You know, our best against their best. And I'd like to see the Cheyenne win. I think a small victory like that might take the edge off some real trouble. It's obvious how close we are to trouble, men. The other day a Cheyenne tried to kill a Crow. These men are frustrated and angry."

"So I let one of them beat me up," Malone said gloomily.

"If you go along with it. I know it's a lot to ask. You

pay the price for my gamble, but that's what I'm asking of you, Malone. I won't order you."

"You don't have to order me, sir. Fightin's nothing new to me. Hell, losin's nothing new. But throwing a fight!"

"I know it's tough to swallow. It could be there'll be some corporal's stripes in this, Malone. I can't promise it, but there could be."

Malone smiled thinly at that. He had had corporal's stripes, plenty of times. They just never seemed to stick. He shrugged. "Hell, I'll do it, sir."

"Good man." Kincaid grinned in return, and poured the dregs of his coffee out to sputter against the coals. "I'll let you know when and where after it's set."

"Sacrifical lamb," Rafferty said after Kincaid had gone.

"Well," Malone said, leaning back, "it truly don't matter, Raff. But throwing a fight! Jesus!"

When he next saw Dancing Horse, Matt brought up the idea for a fight, neglecting to mention, of course, that the Cheyenne was assured a victory.

"I find an enthusiasm for this proposal," the Cheyenne leader said. His face glowed as he turned it over. "Of course, it will take the minds of the weary people from their troubles. Amusement and a lifting of the spirits."

"Then you agree," Matt said, cutting short what had every indication of being a long, flowery speech.

"But of course. This is not what I have come to speak about, Lieutenant Matt Kincaid."

"What's on your mind, Dancing Horse?"

"It has come to me that we will not pass this way again. The trail shall end for us in Oklahoma. And so there is one request, for the sake of my spirit."

"And that is?"

"Tonight we shall pass close to Meadow Falls. A place where my people were buried once. Where once medicine was practiced. I shall nevermore see this place, Lieutenant Matt Kincaid."

"How far is it?" Matt asked cautiously.

"It is to the west," Dancing Horse said, brightening. "Fifteen miles, perhaps."

"A thirty-mile detour in all?"

"Thirty miles for my spirit."

"All right." Matt nodded, and Dancing Horse beamed with satisfaction. "That's not too much to ask for the sake of your spirit. This one time," he admonished.

"Of course, Lieutenant Matt Kincaid. And for that I shall always find gratitude." He turned to go. "I shall tell the people of the great challenge fight."

When Dancing Horse left, he walked with his shoulders set, with a spring in his step, and Matt knew he had done the right thing. The people would have something ahead of them on the long trail to look forward to. A visit to the sacred Meadow Falls and a contest of strength with a white soldier.

Maybe it was not strictly by the book, but as Dancing Horse had said, thirty miles was not far for the sake of a man's spirit.

It was early the following morning when they reached Meadow Falls. A grassy canyon rose into the foothills in tiers of bluffs. Here and there, cedar grew on the higher outcroppings. At the head of the canyon, a wide, veil-thin waterfall fell from level to level over gray, water-polished granite.

Unexpectedly, Dancing Horse asked Matt to accompany him to his sacred grove. They walked upslope along an ancient, narrow trail. The smell of grass was sweet, the sun clear and nearly white, the sound of the waterfall hypnotic, nearly mystical.

Dancing Horse led the way back from the rim toward an ancient stand of white oak. In the center of the oaks was an oval-shaped clearing, the ground here and there still showing the blackening of ancient fires. Dancing Horse was breathing raggedly; he was no longer young. But his face was bright. Perhaps his spirit had been renewed.

Looking to the east, Matt had an impressive view of the

waterfalls, the verdant, deep canyon, and the long plains that stretched out beyond.

Dancing Horse sat crosslegged in the center of the clearing. No chanting, no fire, no shaking of rattles. He simply sat in quiet meditation, watching the sunlight streaming through the oaks, glittering on the water-glazed rocks, deepening the green of the grass, the mossy clefts in the stone of the bluff.

It was a ritual that Kincaid could participate in, and he did so. Seating himself, he put all other thoughts out of his mind—the trek, the combat, the military. He simply sat, thinking of nothing at all. The sun was warm on his back. A blue damselfly hummed past, and the waterfall fell endlessly away.

Neither man spoke as they came down the mountain, but Dancing Horse was in high spirits. In the camp, the Cheyenne had been kept busy clearing a ring for the opponents in the fight.

Now they had cleared a circle some twelve feet across, and Two Fingers sat on his heels, being massaged by Lone Pine. His body had been oiled and it glistened in the sunlight.

Malone stood nearby; his only preparation had been to remove his shirt. Glancing at him, Kincaid noticed the bulging of Malone's shoulders, the corded muscles that ran the length of his spine—indicators of a deal of strength. The man looked more powerful than Kincaid would have guessed, seeing him dressed. Like most powerful men, Malone had a deal of pride. Matt only hoped Malone could put that pride aside long enough to lose this fight.

As if guessing the lieutenant's thoughts, Malone glanced up and winked as Kincaid walked past.

The Cheyenne had begun to gather around the clearing, and Kincaid's men were drifting in as well. Malone took a series of deep breaths and shook his arm muscles loose, hanging his head, wriggling his shoulders.

Finally he nodded and strode toward the clearing, where Two Fingers, his oiled skin glistening, waited. In deference to Two Fingers' injured wrist, an agreement had been reached that this would be a one-handed affair. Two Fingers had his splinted, bandaged hand strapped to his waist. Malone simply reached behind his own back and gripped his belt.

Malone entered the ring to a chorus of whistling, jeering, and the cheers of the soldiers. There were no formal rules, and so there was no referee. The last man standing was to be the winner.

Two Fingers stood waiting, his hair knotted on the back of his skull, his dark eyes haughty. Malone spat and walked to meet him.

Malone was undeniably the stronger of the two men, but it didn't take long for Two Fingers to demonstrate that he was by far the quicker.

As Malone toed the mark, Two Fingers kicked out with his left foot and then his right, in a sort of dance step. The first blow caught Malone below the knee, the second caught him on the ribcage.

Grunting, Malone backstepped. Then, grinning, he came in, his hand in front of him, clawing for Two Fingers' bobbing head. They circled warily, measuring each other. Two Fingers tried another kick, but Malone slapped his ankle as the foot came up, and Two Fingers was knocked slightly off balance.

Suddenly impatient, Two Fingers howled and drove at Malone, his head low, his legs churning. Malone slugged at the Cheyenne's jaw, grazed it, and grabbed his hair as Two Fingers took them both head over heels.

Malone landed on his back, rolled free, and came up in time to avoid a kick by Two Fingers that would have taken his head off.

Malone was not so good with his feet, but he managed to follow a feint with his fist with a stunning kick, which caught Two Fingers painfully on the hip.

Two Fingers fought back angrily. He clawed at Malone's eyes, his fingers like talons, and Malone had to throw up a forearm to knock his hand away. To Kincaid, Malone seemed to be getting angry—the gouging attempt hadn't set right with the soldier.

Now Malone moved inside. He gripped Two Fingers by the throat and backheeled him. Two Fingers went down in a heap and Malone kicked him twice in the ribs before Two Fingers rolled away, the dust he raised drifting across the clearing to sift through the observers.

Two Fingers crouched, came in, and met with one of Malone's right hooks, and Malone had a good one. Two Fingers went to his knees, but was quickly up and circling.

Malone had blood in his eyes and Kincaid was starting to worry, but the Cheyenne warrior was far from finished. With a yowl he launched himself at Malone's knees, driving him back.

On the ground once more, they rolled and swung wild punches, Malone tagging Two Fingers on the ear, Two Fingers countering with a stiff shot to Malone's eye. Malone hooked two rights to Two Fingers' ribs, driving him off, but as he tried to follow, the Cheyenne shoved his moccasined foot into his nose, bringing a flow of crimson blood.

The Indians cheered at the sight of the blood, and Malone felt rage building up inside of him. He grabbed at Two Fingers and tried to throw him with a hip lock, but the Cheyenne's oiled body slipped through his grip, and Malone was left open to a jarring uppercut.

Malone's head snapped back, his teeth clacking together, and Two Fingers moved confidently in, kicking twice before trying a jab to Malone's head.

Malone simply bobbed away from that and brought his own right in underneath, landing hard on the Cheyenne's chest, above the heart. Dropping down, Malone moved in, hooking and butting up with his head. His skull caught Two Fingers' chin and the Indian went down.

Two Fingers rolled to his knees and got slowly up. Malone stood away, beckoning to him, his face and chest smeared with his own blood, his hair hanging damply in his eyes.

Across the clearing he caught sight of Kincaid, and Malone at first averted his eyes. Caught up in the spirit of the fight, it was against all of his instincts to quit.

But his eyes met Kincaid's and held. The lieutenant was not angry or visibly disturbed. Quietly, he simply reminded Malone of a promise made, and Malone nodded imperceptibly.

Two Fingers staggered toward him, keeping Malone at bay with a series of little kicks at the knees and groin. Malone moved back with each crow-hop that Two Fingers took, until he was near the edge of the ring. Just for a moment in the crowd he caught a glimpse of Spring Walk standing there, her dark eyes unreadable.

Hell, he thought, *let's have done with it.*

He went straight into Two Fingers, hooking to the head, driving up with a knee that was deflected off the Indian's thigh.

Two Fingers shot out a good stiff jab, and Malone's head rocked back. The blood began to flow again from his nose and mouth. He thought a tooth or two had come loose with that one, but he paid it no mind.

He simply waded in, swinging and missing. Two Fingers chopped a right that Malone blocked, then Malone deliberately dropped his guard and a second right from the Cheyenne got through cleanly. Malone was rocked back on his heels.

He went down in a heap. Two Fingers stood over him, taunting him, and Malone peered up at the Cheyenne. Then he simply closed his eyes and lay back, sprawling in the dust of the arena.

He stayed there, listening to the cheers, the war whoops, the laughter. Feet rushed past him, and through a slit between his eyelids he saw Two Fingers hoisted onto their shoulders, and then they rushed him away, their fists raised victoriously.

A shadow cut out the sunlight and Malone peeked up. Someone was leaning over him. It was Rafferty, squatting on his heels.

"Come on and get up, champ," Rafferty said with a grin.

"Unless you want me to go get some water and make it look even better."

"All right." Malone got to his knees and stayed there for a time, shaking his head. He heard footsteps and in surprise, saw Two Fingers returning. "Damned if I'll throw it again," Malone said, coming stiffly to his feet, but there was no need to do that.

Two Fingers stuck out his good hand and smiled through his battered, puffy lips. "Good fight, Malone."

Despite himself, Malone took the hand and shook it, somehow, in a way he could not explain, feeling better about having lost than he had after many a winning brawl.

Two Fingers walked away, his back straight, into the embrace of his tribe, and Malone shrugged. He turned with Rafferty and saw her still standing there.

Spring Walk. She simply stared at him for a long minute and then strode past him without speaking, to join her tribe in its celebration.

"Kincaid's never going to know how much this fight cost me," Malone grumbled as Rafferty gave him his shirt and a canteen.

Glancing toward Kincaid, Malone saw that he was not alone. A man in range clothes, sitting a blaze-faced roan, was in close conversation with Lieutenant Kincaid. He had slipped up beside Matt as the fight reached its climax, and Kincaid had not even been aware of his presence until the man drawled, "Looks like your boy's gettin' the worst of it."

Startled, Matt had turned around, missing the final blow that had sent Malone sprawling. He looked the cattleman over, for cattleman he was, no doubt.

A big-shouldered, long-jawed man with an unkempt mustache, he had thoughtful dark eyes beneath heavy black eyebrows.

"Surprise you, Lieutenant?" the man asked with amusement.

"You did that, Mr.—"

"Huggins, Lieutenant. John Allan Huggins." He spat a stream of tobacco and watched as Rafferty gave Malone a canteen of water, which the soldier poured over his head and shoulders. "I thought I surprised you. Of course, you folks surprised the hell out of me, being up here." He looked around, his face thoughtful. "Now, I'd much appreciate it if you'd all pull up stakes and get the hell out of here."

"Do what?"

"This is my land, Lieutenant. I guess maybe I could stand a few bluecoats on it, but by God I can't stomach Cheyenne trampling my grass."

"We are only camping for the night, sir. Then, I assure you—"

"You ain't campin' the night, sir," Huggins said, wagging his head as if with deep sorrow. "I said off and I mean off. I mean now."

"If I could explain—"

Kincaid was interrupted again. "I do the explainin', Lieutenant. And I've done all I'm goin' to do. You're on my ranch and I'm orderin' you off. Now."

Kincaid was fighting back his anger. Huggins sat his horse quietly, a self-confident, calm man who was used to brooking no contradiction.

"All right," Kincaid said finally. "We'll pull out, though it's damned inconvenient."

"Inconvenient to have you here," Huggins said mildly. "I'd have to figure a way to keep my boys from comin' over here and killin' a few savages."

"Now wait a minute!"

Don't like threats?" Huggins smiled. "I don't like makin' 'em, but it's a fact. Get out or get shot at. Matter of fact," he said as an afterthought, "I might have to bill the army for the grass your horses are chewin' anyway."

"I said we will leave, Mr. Huggins," Matt said, restraining himself only with great difficulty. "Tonight. Now."

"See you do," Huggins said. He spat again, into the dust not six inches from the toe of Kincaid's boot. "And by the way, Lieutenant, that's my property to the south, as well. For the next twenty miles. I don't want to see you or your Injuns anywhere on it."

"We'd have to circle back and go around the mountains!" Matt exploded.

"Yes, sir. I guess maybe you would. But I'll tell you now, you'll fare better that way than trying to take them cutthroat Cheyenne across any land that belongs to John Allan Huggins." He winked, "Good advice well meant, Lietenant. See you take it."

Matt watched him turn his roan and ride at a walk down the long, grassy canyon. Corporal Wojensky had been standing at a respectful distance, watching and listening. Now he walked up to his lieutenant.

"You heard that?" Kincaid asked Wojensky.

The corporal nodded. "Most of it. What are you going to do, sir?"

"Do?" Matt Kincaid seemed surprised by the question. He looked steadily at Wojensky and told him. "We're army, Corporal. I've got my orders. We'll go through and hope the man has sense enough to stay off us. If he doesn't"—Kincaid smiled bitterly—"well, we've got ourselves a nice little war coming."

eight ─────────────────

They trailed out before sunset, the Cheyenne still in good spirits, Matt Kincaid deeply concerned. He sent the Crow scouts ahead of the party. Now they would start earning their pay. Somewhere ahead, Huggins would be watching and waiting, and when Kincaid swung the party south, deeper into his land, the fuse would be lit.

The troopers rode with their rifles at the ready, their eyes constantly searching the surrounding countryside. For the first five miles they would be riding the flats between two low lines of foothills. It was a bad tactical situation, but then it was a situation that allowed for no tactics. Kincaid glanced back at the long line of horses, men, dogs, women, and kids, and he knew there was no way in hell they would ever be able to run.

If it came to a fight, they were ducks on a pond. And it was John Allan Huggins' pond.

"I can't see a way out of it." Captain Conway shook his head again and placed the reports down, squaring them to match the corner of his desk. Ben Cohen stood at parade rest before his commanding officer.

"I certainly couldn't," Cohen answered. "I was hoping maybe between us we could find a way to keep the hook from biting too deep. Kip Schoendienst has the makings of a good soldier, sir. He truly does."

"We may never be able to prove that," Captain Conway

said with resignation. "Incredible bad luck—getting picked up by regimental MPs."

"Bad luck seems attracted to certain men. Schoendienst's one of them. How many times have we had a soldier take a drink too many?" Cohen shook his head. "The poor dumb son of a bitch," the first soldier muttered.

"How's he taking it?"

"The way any man looking down the barrel of a gun takes it, sir. He has given up hope, I suppose you'd say."

"Then he's smarter than we are," Warner Conway said. "I haven't been able to bring myself to give up quite yet."

"What's the latest you can delay the court-martial, sir?"

"The regimental inspector will be here in two days, Sergeant." Cohen stood. "I will have to send a report back to the TJA with him."

"Yes, the inspection—another sore spot."

"Your men will pass it, Sergeant," Conway said with a confidence Sergeant Cohen didn't share.

"If we do, the inspector's blind."

They walked out together into the sunlight. "I wonder how Kincaid's getting along with his Indian charges," Captain Cohen said.

"That's likely a piece of cake, sir, wouldn't you think? Leading a band of tame Indians to the Nation." Cohen was thoughtful, wishing he were on that Oklahoma Trail, where there were no inspections, no Kip Schoendienst.

"Where in God's name did he come by that?" Captain Conway said abruptly.

Cohen's head lifted. He too saw Mr. John Fairchild, Jr. leading a white gelding from the paddock. The horse's tail was braided neatly. It was a big animal, a hand taller than the regulation bays. An officer was allowed to have his own horse, of course, providing he paid for the care and feeding of it. But for most junior officers, it was financially out of the question. It amounted to nothing more than showboating.

"Well, I suppose he wants to be different," Cohen said

96

with a shrug. They watched as Fairchild mounted and put the gelding through a series of fancy paces.

"He is that," Conway said softly. At Cohen's glance he explained, "Different."

"He'll make a good officer, sir," Cohen said. "He's got the bloodlines."

"Yes," Conway sighed, "he does. He may make it, Sergeant, but the waiting period is going to be a little rough. I believe I might have the man transferred—if I could think of a commander I dislike enough to do it to."

"More trouble?" Cohen didn't usually ask about the affairs of the outpost's officers, but Conway seemed to want to talk.

"You mean besides ruining Cambury's wedding, bringing Gus Olsen up on false charges, harassing the enlisted men, and cheating at cards?" Conway asked. "No, not much else."

Cohen smiled, but turned his head away—the captain was hurting with this. He wanted the kid to work out nearly as much as old John Fairchild probably did. But it wasn't working. There was some common decency lacking in Lieutenant Fairchild, some arrogance toward his fellowman that would keep him from being a good officer, or even a decent man, until it was somehow deflated. They only hoped that the man would learn somehow, and learn quickly enough, because John Fairchild, on that big white gelding, was riding hard toward disaster.

Cohen left the captain and walked toward the gate. Trueblood owed the sutler money, and Pop Evans was crying about it. It was only five dollars, but a man could find the ground opening up under his feet real quick from indebtedness.

Trueblood was on gate guard and he promised Cohen that come payday, Evans would be first. Satisfied, Ben walked to the sutler's.

He opened the door, and a tinny-sounding brass bell rang. After a minute, Pop Evans peered out of the storeroom. His pinched face brightened with assumed enthusiasm as he saw Cohen and came out to the counter, offering a bony hand.

Cohen took it briefly, tilted back his hat, and leaned his forearms on the counter, eyeing Evan's stock. "I talked to Trueblood," Ben said. "He promises you're first in line come payday."

"Good." Evans rubbed his hands together, producing a dry, leathery sound. "I hate to see these boys get in trouble."

Sure you do, Cohen thought. *That's why you make a hundred-percent profit on everything from boots to soap.*

Credit only required a shake of the hand with Pop Evans. But come payday he was hovering like a vulture, and God help the man who didn't pay. He had a hook set deep; no man could be discharged until his debts were settled with Evans—army regulations.

He was free with credit and he had the only beer for fifty miles. Three-point-two, by regulation, but that didn't slow the sales. A man drinks what there is. No one, Evans or the soldiers, would ever admit it, but there was whiskey passing over that counter as well, and Cohen damn well knew it.

"What can I do for you, Sergeant Cohen? I've got some blue calico in. You might tell Maggie." He reached under the counter and shoved a handful of cigars toward Cohen. He wanted the first shirt on his team. Cohen looked at the cigars, but left them.

"I think you've got Maggie's shopping allowance already this month, Evans. I'll tell her though."

Pop chuckled and nodded, as if he and Cohen shared some secret about womenfolk. All the time, however, his little shoe-button eyes were calculating, measuring. He knew Ben Cohen well enough to know that something was up; Cohen was hardly a man to engage in idle gossip.

Cohen was doing his own measuring. He wanted this to sound plausible and larcenous—he wanted to bait that hook carefully before he dangled it in front of Pop's greedy little eyes.

"Been down to the agency lately?" Cohen asked, lifting his eyes to the door as if exercising caution. Evans was quick to pick up on the seeming furtiveness. His voice lowered conspiratorially.

"Not lately. I'm not licensed to trade with the Indians, you know."

"That's what I recalled." Ben shrugged heavily. "Too bad." He straightened his hat and nodded. "Well, I guess I'll be seeing you, Pop."

"Wait a minute." Pop Evans came around the counter. "You didn't ask that question for nothing, Ben."

Cohen shrugged again. "No—but we can't do business. Might as well forget it."

It was Pop Evans who now glanced around. No one was nearby. "Maybe I could give you some advice, Ben, even if I can't help you outright. Now, it's got to be business. I know you're not shooting the breeze. What do you say we have some coffee—the real stuff, no chicory—and knock it around a little."

Ben hesitated just long enough, then nodded. "All right. Let's knock it around."

Evans got a coffeepot and two cups, and they sat together at a table in the storeroom; Pop left the door open so he could see anyone entering the store. The sutler's eyes were frankly interested. They gleamed, and as Ben's story went on, they glittered like gold eagles.

"What it is," Ben said in a low, confidential voice, "is that I was down at the agency yesterday, talking to Jake Ten Knives—you know old Jake."

"He's a damned thief," Pop spat.

"Maybe, but he's good at his job. What he's got ..." Ben glanced toward the door again. "Furs, Pop. Not the moth-eaten, thin stuff we've been seeing lately, but prime stuff from the high-up mountains."

"Furs?"

"Otter, silver fox, beaver pelts. Thickest damned furs I've seen in years. Must've been a hell of a cold winter up there. So somehow Jake Ten Knives has come by 'em. I heard a nasty little story about how, but we'll let that lie for now."

"So Jake wants to sell?"

"He *wants* to," Ben said, leaning forward, his voice a whisper, "but to who? Not to no damned Indians—they can't afford 'em. And the thing is, Jake can't bring 'em out on the open market. Like I say, there's some trouble behind this."

"How'd you come to find out about them, Ben?"

"He approached me, Pop. I had a look at the furs. I'm telling you, they're rich. Must be five thousand dollars' worth if there's a nickel's worth."

"Why cut me in?" Pop asked suspiciously.

"He wants five hundred. Five Hundred, Pop! It's nothing compared to what they're worth, but Jake wants to unload 'em pronto. Even so, five hundred is a fair piece of change to me. And," he confided, "the army doesn't look kindly on its NCOs trading . . . suspicious goods with the Indians."

"Stolen."

"I didn't say that." Ben lifted a protesting hand. "I don't know that it's so. I don't want to know."

Pop's words were cautious, but his hands clenched and unclenched with the reflexes of greed. His eyes positively glittered.

"Say I did go in—and I'm not sure about that, Ben, you know I wouldn't want to be involved in anything shady— how would we split it?"

"Fifty-fifty. I'll put in two hundred and a half. You come in for the same amount and we clear five thousand, minimum!"

"I might consider it," Pop said, leaning back so that only his fingertips rested on the table. "Of course, I'd have to give it a deal of thought, check out Jake's ownership."

"There's damn little time for that," Ben said, shaking his head. "Jake wants those furs gone from the agency by the day after tomorrow, no later. Were I you, Pop, I'd take a look-see. Take a wagon with you in case you buy, and I'm sure you will."

"You'll give me your two-fifty?"

"When you get back, if you buy."

"I'd have to close up the store," Pop said. "That would cost me."

"Leave it closed, then—hell, man, we're talking big money."

It was a long, agonizing minute before Pop Evans said, "All right. On your say-so, Ben, I'll have a look. I'll leave in the morning."

"You won't be sorry," Ben said, shoving his chair back. "Neither of us will."

They shook hands, sealing the bargain, and Pop escorted him to the door. He stood watching as Cohen ambled across the parade, and for a moment he had second thoughts. True, in Pop's philosophy everyone was out to make a buck, but somehow Cohen had never seemed the wheeler-dealer type. But then, army pay wasn't much, and a man has to be on the lookout for opportunity.

Besides, he thought reassuringly, what possible motive could Cohen have for pulling a fast one? If the furs were no good, Pop wouldn't buy. The most he could lose was a little business. Twenty-five hundred as his share! He fed that amount mentally into his books, and liked the feeling.

Cohen walked into the orderly room, and his eyes settled on the clerk sitting there sorting dispatches. Four Eyes glanced up apprehensively.

"You know, Four Eyes, you sit too much."

Four Eyes shrugged. "It's the job, Sarge."

"I think you need to get out a little."

Four Eyes watched apprehensively as Cohen circled his desk. "Yes, son, you're getting a little pale, a little puny. How about taking a little ride?"

"A ride, Sarge? Where?"

"Down to the agency. I've got a message for you to deliver. You know Jake Ten Knives?"

They rode through the night, using the Crow scouts as outriders. Twenty miles, Huggins had said. Kincaid meant to make twenty miles this night. They were obviously nearer the home ranch now. They passed cattle along the riverbeds. White faces appeared suddenly out of the shadows and turned, bawling, to run into the brush.

Twenty miles was a long march under any circumstances. Now the Cheyenne dragged their heels, wanting to set up camp, to eat, to nurse their babies, but Kincaid kept them moving.

"You will kill them!" Dancing Horse complained.

"Not me, Dancing Horse. But there are some men out there who likely would, given the chance."

"Then give us back our weapons."

"No."

That was the last thing Matt wanted to do. Give those Cheyenne their guns, and who was to say how far they might go after shooting a cowboy. Matt tightened his jaw and shook his head, refusing to argue anymore, and Dancing Horse fell back.

"How far you reckon, Lieutenant?" Wojensky wondered.

"Not far enough," Matt replied.

"I'll try to get them to pick up the pace."

Wojensky had little luck with that, except for the Contraries. "Stop!" he ordered them. "Sit down." And they rushed doggedly forward.

The crescent moon slid slowly westward. Kincaid's horse was laboring and he could hear the Cheyenne children crying. Still they traveled on, Kincaid pushing them all to the limits of their ability.

The moon was lost behind the far Rocky Mountains, and the land was growing gray with the light of false dawn, when they came upon them.

They were strung out upon a grassy rise—dark, menacing silhouettes in a perfect rank. Kincaid counted twenty in all, and he knew it was time for a reckoning. He slowed his bay—there was no point in hurrying now—and raised the rifle in his hand, the signal for hostile contact.

He heard the clatter of weapons being readied, heard the

horses of his soldiers rushing to form up behind him. Dawn broke free of the night and backlighted the men on the rise with pale orange.

"Tell Dancing Horse to hold his people back," Kincaid said. His voice was oddly tight, as if he were short of breath.

"Yes, sir." Wojensky wheeled back and halted the Cheyenne.

Returning, he formed up, and with Kincaid at the head of the column, they rode up the long, dew-frosted knoll. Kincaid formed his men into a picket line and they moved ominously toward the line of sunrise-silhouetted cowhands, matched nearly man for man.

As they neared, the sun emerged as a white, shimmering ball from below the black horizon. A thin line of brilliant gold edged the mountain peaks beyond. Huggins shook himself free of his formation and rode slowly forward to meet Kincaid, a second man siding him.

Matt halted his bay fifty yards off, waiting. Wojensky was twenty feet behind him and to his left, his Springfield across his saddlebow.

Huggins wore a slicker, as did the man with him. Each carried a rifle, a Winchester repeater. Kincaid tugged his hat lower against the sun and waited, listening to the clumping of the approaching horses' hooves.

They halted before Matt, and it was Huggins who spoke:

"I thought you were a man of some sense."

"I'd hoped *you* were, Huggins," Kincaid replied. "We're coming through, by the authority of the United States government."

"The hell you are," the man siding Huggins said. Matt glanced at him. A tall, thin kid with a lean face and a surly set to his lips. Matt ignored him.

"We had an understanding," Huggins said.

"No, sir. *You* had an understanding. *I* had my orders."

"Orders be damned, you'll turn around and get the hell off of here, or be shot!" Huggins said this sternly, but he was in control of his temper—perhaps he never showed temper, Matt thought, studying the tightly composed face of John Allan Huggins. But he didn't doubt for a minute that Huggins was in dead earnest.

The kid beside him bore a faint resemblance to the old man, but he had no such control over his emotions. He fidgeted and shifted in the saddle, his hand white as he gripped the rifle tightly. He wanted to shoot, this one, to see a war. Kincaid wondered if he wanted to *be* shot. His type never considered that possibility until it happened, and then they groveled and cried like babies.

"I figure we're closer now to your southern boundary than the northern," Matt said. "Makes no sense to me to turn back."

"It does to me. You were ordered off."

"How far is it?" Matt persisted. "Two miles?"

"Three."

"You'd start a war over that?"

"Damn right we would," the kid said.

"Shut up, Kenny." Huggins smiled, but it was a grim smile. "My nephew don't know when to shut up, but what he says is right. I'd fight. I been fighting for this land for twenty years, Lieutenant. Cheyenne, Arapaho, whites—I fought 'em all and I'm still sittin' here."

"Not for long," Kincaid said, and Huggin's smile evaporated. "There's only two things that can come out of this, Huggins. One: you win. Two: you lose.

"If you lose, you'll likely be planted under this grass of yours and you'll not have to worry about any of it anymore. If you win, it'll only be for as long as it takes reinforcements to reach here. Likely your house will be fired, and then you'll be hung. You and all of your hands. If you managed to get away, federal marshals would hunt you down. Maybe you'd get away. But you'd have to hide. You damn sure would never see Wyoming and this ranch again. Is your pride worth that much? We'll be off your property in three miles. One hour."

"Go to hell," Kenny growled.

"Shut up," Huggins said again.

"You're not giving in to him, Uncle John!" the kid said in sheer exasperation. He wanted blood, wanted it bad.

"If a man thinks about it . . ." Huggins said with a sigh. He looked behind him at his waiting cowboys, beyond Kincaid to study the line of soldiers, the Cheyenne farther back. "It don't make a hell of a lot of sense."

"Uncle John!"

"The man's right. Let's get home to breakfast, Kenny."

"Like hell!" Kenny's rifle came up and he fired from the hip. The bullet whipped past Matt Kincaid's ear, and Matt raked his bay's flanks with his spurs.

The bay leaped forward and Matt launched himself from the saddle. He hit Kenny Huggins square and knocked him from his horse's back. Together the two men hit the ground and rolled down the hill, Huggins's horse dancing away in panic.

Kenny, in a frothing fury, bit, kicked, and swung fists that bounced off Kincaid's back. They came to their feet together, nearly under the hoofs of the soldiers' horses.

Kenny Huggins was positively shrieking with rage, cursing, pawing at Kincaid. Matt stuck a left into the kid's face, measuring him, and then arched a beautiful right over the kid's guard, dropping him cold to the grass.

Matt swung around, his hand going to his service revolver, but Huggins had not moved, nor had the line of waiting cowboys.

Panting, Matt yanked the semiconscious Kenny to his feet and, carrying him by his collar, propelled him toward Huggins.

"Damn, Kenny," the old man said sorrowfully, "that was pitiful, son. Cain't you even fight?" He turned to Kincaid. "Ride on through," he said. "But let me get out of sight first. I don't want to have to look at them raggedy Cheyenne. Another thing," he said after turning his horse. "I *will* send a bill to the army for the grass you're ruining."

Then Huggins was gone, and the line of cowboys disappeared over the hill. Kenny Huggins tracked down his horse in the valley below and, whipping the startled animal on the head with his hat, he followed his uncle.

"That was close," Wojensky said. He held the reins to the lieutenant's horse, and as Kincaid turned, he handed him his hat.

"The man has sense," Kincaid said in response. Wojensky took it that he meant Huggins. "He just doesn't like to hear the word 'no'—probably doesn't hear it much."

Kincaid stepped into the stirrups and waited. When he could no longer see Huggins, he moved them out. "Three miles, Wojensky. Tell the Cheyenne only three more miles, and then we'll camp."

"Yes, sir."

"Sir?"

It was Malone who spoke, and he turned toward the private, returning his salute. "Yes, what is it, Malone?"

"Just wanted to tell the lieutenant—after what I saw, I reckon the lieutenant can handle his own fighting from now on. We won't be losing much."

Then he grinned, saluted, and returned to the right flank. Kincaid sat smiling for a minute, catching his breath. Then he waved his hand and they moved on out, a little farther down that long Oklahoma Trail.

nine ─────────────────

At the rap on the doorframe, Captain Conway's head came up.

"Come in, John." he said.

John Fairchild, Jr. swaggered into the room, snapped a salute, and stood waiting expectantly.

"I'm going to give you a chance to take a patrol out, John," Warner Conway said. He looked at the young man before him, into those pale, haughty eyes, trying to understand him.

"I'm looking forward to it," Fairchild replied.

"I know you are. I'm giving you Sergeant Olsen and Windy Madalian here." He nodded to the man in the corner.

Fairchild glanced at the lean civilian, clad in greasy buckskins, his hair a tangle, his cheek distended by a wad of tobacco. He nodded slightly, and Windy nodded back.

"A scout? You expect I shall have to do some tracking then, sir?"

"No. A scout is more than a tracker, John. Especially a good one, and Windy is the best. He knows the land, knows the Indians—their tendencies, their habits, when they will fight and when they will run. Listen to him; he knows more of the Cheyenne than we ever will. He's been all of his adult life on the plains."

Fairchild nodded politely and smiled. His attention actually seemed to be drifting, Conway noted with disturbance. He rose and walked to the map on his wall, explaining the patrol's mission.

"We've been playing hide-and-seek with a group of a dozen young bucks, agency jumpers. Last evening they burned a deserted house up along the Trinity, and the people are beginning to howl again."

Conway paused, expecting a question. There was none from Fairchild, so he went on. Windy was watching through narrowed eyes from his corner chair.

"You'll have to sweep through this entire sector, John." Conway's palm arced across the map. "I really don't expect there's a real chance of an offensive move by these renegades." He glanced at Windy, who nodded in agreement.

"And if there is contact, sir?"

"If there is contact, try to peacefully arrest these men and escort them back to the agency. They really don't mean anything by all of this, John. Not these bucks. It's just that the old ways of proving manhood—by fighting, counting coup—are still vivid in their minds, while the opportunities for such feats of bravery are now severely limited.

"And so they stir up a little trouble. Steal a few horses, burn an old barn. They want to ride back to their tribe with tales of courage to relate, to impress the women."

"The old ones talk," Windy said, speaking up for the first time, "of battles with the Sioux, the Crow, with the white soldiers. They sit around the lodge, wearing their eagle feathers and the scars of the Sun Dance. The young bucks, they got nothing to show, nothing to brag on. This kind of monkeyshinin' goes on all the time. Mostly it don't mean a thing."

"But it rattles the settlers," Captain Conway added. "Many of them have been through bloody battles with the Cheyenne, and have lost loved ones. Horses are dear on the plains, and they don't like losing them to a bunch of Indians who are supposedly restricted to the agency."

"I understand fully, sir. The least possible force."

"That is the crux of it, John. Windy? Anything else to add?"

"We don't know much else, Captain. No, that's it."

"All right then." Conway rose. "Good luck to you. Keep your eyes open and your heads down."

Windy picked up his big Spencer rifle, which was encased in a buckskin sheath, and nodded and went out, moving in that catlike way he had.

Fairchild hesitated. "Is it necessary for Sergeant Olsen to be under my command, Captain?" he asked.

"He's the most experienced man I have available, John."

"There has been, ah—a difference of opinion between us, sir."

"Gus Olsen is a soldier. He will obey your orders, John. He has seen more Indians than you have imagined, and in the event you are incapacitated, he would be a fully capable second-in-command. Yes, I want Olsen with you this first time out."

"Very good, sir," Fairchild said, saluting.

But Conway could tell it wasn't "very good" in Fairchild's mind. He sat at his desk in deep thought after Fairchild had gone. Was this the right thing? It had to be done. Fairchild had been out half a dozen times now with Taylor or Fitzgerald. It was time to find out if the kid had the stuff.

After all, he thought, reassuring himself, it wasn't as if this were a full-combat situation. A handful of young renegades who would likely turn tail and run back to the agency at the sight of their first bluecoat...

Maybe. Warner Conway returned to his correspondence, not quite able to shake the nagging, uncomfortable feeling in the back of his mind.

Hours later, he rose and went to the front door of the headquarters building, to watch as Fairchild formed up his men and led them out through the gate, the dust of their departure rising into the clear air.

He watched until they were only dark, indistinct forms

against the long dry grass of the prairie, and then he turned back toward his office. It was done, there was no point in worrying about it.

The days grew warmer, the weather drier, as they trailed inexorably southward. By Matt's reckoning, they were well into Colorado now. The Crow were out looking for the Republican River, which Kincaid intended to follow into Kansas, assuring the party of water.

Here and there now, they saw small settlements, which Kincaid scrupulously avoided, and cattle browsing on the open range.

"And still the land grows drier," Dancing Horse said, looking across the golden brown of the plains. "Until we reach the Nation of Indians—where I am sure the land must be parched stone and storms of dust where nothing grows, where no buffalo can survive."

"Was there something you wanted?" Matt asked. The speech was not a new one, and under the glaring sun, Kincaid was too impatient to listen to it again.

"We are in need of supplies," Dancing Horse said. With the barest of smiles he added, "This time it is true, Lieutenant Kincaid."

"This time I know it is true," Kincaid said. His own men were on short rations now, and like it or not, he was going to have to approach the next town they neared with his ragged legion.

Iron Owl drifted back in shortly after noon, reported spotting the Republican, now forty miles distant, and advised Matt that there was indeed a town some twenty miles ahead and to the east.

"Very well. We'll swing that way, camp before dark, and replenish our supplies."

There was a very good chance that the townspeople would not like the Cheyenne camping near them, Matt knew, but they didn't have to like it. The long trail was beginning to make him edgy, and the run-in with Huggins hadn't helped any.

That could damn well have turned into a bloodbath, and Kincaid knew it.

The town was called Gatlin. Not much of a town, but it contained a whole hell of a lot of cattle and cowboys.

That was enough to give Matt second thoughts. Drinking men are apt to be reckless men, and there's no harder drinker than a cowboy after a drive.

The Cheyenne camp was set up as dusk settled, purpling the land. The cookfires dotted the dark hillside with cones of red. Matt took the time to shave before riding in, and it was while he was scraping off the last of his beard that he got the bad news.

In his mirror he saw the sober face of Dancing Horse, and he turned, waving the Cheyenne leader into his tent.

"What's happened?" Matt wanted to know immediately, for it was obvious from Dancing Horse's expression that something had.

"Our supplies are low," the old warrior said.

"Yes, we've been through that. I'm going to purchase some now."

"Our supplies were low, and providence offered an occasion to replenish the empty larder of the wandering Cheyenne . . ."

"Damn it, Dancing Horse, what's happened?"

"Two young men killed a steer to eat. It is roasting now."

"They butchered a steer? Did anyone see them?"

"They think not." Dancing Horse was uneasy. So was Kincaid. All they needed was for the Cheyenne to start butchering whatever range cattle they came upon.

Matt thought quickly. "Tell them to bury the hide. And bring them to me immediately."

"They are here, Lieutenant." Dancing Horse nodded toward the tent flap. "I had them brought along."

"Get them."

Dancing Horse went to the flap and called out. In a moment they appeared. Two young men, in their late teens, Matt guessed, were brought forward by two Crooked Lance soldiers.

"Stick is his name," Dancing Horse said. "And the other is called Sky Bear."

The two stared expressionlessly at Kincaid. The one called Stick had his arms folded on his chest. The other, the bigger of the two, still had blood on his hands from his butchering.

"You have brought trouble to us," Kincaid said, walking to within a pace of the two warriors. "You have taken a cattleman's beef. If it is discovered, there will be trouble."

"Let it come," Stick said. "I am not afraid."

Dancing Horse shouted at him, and the youth fell into a brooding silence. Kincaid wiped back his hair and slowly said, "I know you are not afraid. That is not the point."

"The animal was free on the plains," Sky Bear said with a deep shrug that lifted his shoulders to his ears, "and we saw it. We killed it."

"That was not a buffalo," Matt said patiently. "It was a man's property. A cow a man has fed and watched over."

"They are not so stupid," Dancing Horse said sharply. "They know the difference between a buffalo and a white man's steer. They simply did not care if trouble came upon the tribe, if their fathers and mothers were hurt because of their foolishness."

Stick appeared slightly shamed, Sky Bear not at all. One of the Crooked Lances thumped the boy hard between his shoulder blades.

"It would be only through the wildest coincidence that anyone finds out about this," Kincaid told Dancing Horse. "Once the hide is buried, see that all of the steer is eaten, even if it has to be given to the dogs. But there can be no more of this. No more!"

"No more," Stick said, but his eyes had that sullen impudence still. Sky Bear said nothing.

"Now take them and punish them," Matt said.

"Me? You allow it?" Dancing Horse touched his fingertips to his chest in amazement.

"You. Whatever punishment I give, they will resent. Some Cheyenne may think me too lenient, but others will think I am cruel. You may decide, Dancing Horse. These are your people."

Dancing Horse muttered something to the Crooked Lances, and they spun the two young men around by the shoulders, taking them outside. Dancing Horse, still wearing an expression of amazement, followed.

Corporal Wojensky was waiting outside as Matt emerged from his tent. Dusk painted the plains with deep purple and highlights of faded red. Quail sang off in the long grass, and a Cheyenne dog bayed mournfully.

"I'm riding into Gatlin, Corporal. Notify Rafferty and MacArthur that they're to make two packhorses ready and come along."

"Yes, sir." Wojensky saluted and went off to find the two soldiers. Kincaid stood watching the Indian camp. Smoke from a dozen fires lifted lazily into the sky. In the largest tipi, that of Dancing Horse, a council was being held. Those two young braves would be punished swiftly and imaginatively.

When Rafferty and MacArthur arrived, each leading a packhorse, Matt swung up, leaving Wojensky in charge, advising him to set the night guard out farther than usual, and above all to keep the Cheyenne in camp.

"Anything else, sir?"

"Yes, keep our soldiers off those Cheyenne ladies, will you?" he asked with a fragment of a smile.

Wojensky nodded and promised to try. The shadows stretched long before the horses as Kincaid led his supply party out, and by the time they had traveled a mile, the shadows had spread and been absorbed by the plains, and were no more.

Gatlin boasted two intersecting streets, a dozen-odd false-fronted frame buildings, some low, plank-walled houses dotted iregularly about the town, a few tents with plank floors, a yellow brick bank—and fifteen saloons. The brands of half the cattle outfits in Texas were visible on the ranks of cow ponies tied up at the hitch rails.

As they trailed up the dusty street, they heard glass breaking, heard the mingled laughter, shrieks, and roars of drunken revelry. A drunken cowboy sat square in the middle of Main Street, his eyes dazed and bewildered. From across town, smoke rose from the stack of a locomotive, and they heard the bawling of cattle from the full-packed loading pens.

"Busy little burg," Rafferty observed dryly.

"It's booming. Now."

These towns, which sprung up like mushrooms on the plains along the line of the railroad tracks, had a way of booming, flowering briefly, then dying, as the tracks passed them by. In another year, perhaps, there would be no Gatlin, but the town was making the best of it while it lasted.

A cowboy rolled out of the front door of a saloon, and was followed immediately by a second man. They rolled down the street in a wild, nearly harmless brawl.

The crossroads general store was open, occupied by a few cowhands buying jeans and boots. Kincaid walked past them to the counter, where two men—an older, nearly bald storekeeper and a heavy, slack-jowled redhead—rummaged in the till, or shouted to the storeroom. Kincaid fell in line behind a whiskey- and cow-smelling man with bowlegs, and waited.

Two drunken cowhands staggered into the store, arguing. Suddenly they were quiet, and Matt heard one of them say quite seriously, "Jesus, they called the army in. Let's hit the trail."

He turned toward them, watched them stumble toward the door, and then it was his turn at the counter. "Gave them two a fright," the thin storekeeper said.

"Bad consciences," Matt replied. He shoved his list across the counter, and the storekeeper's eyes lifted toward him with surprise.

"You're feeding an army, aren't you?"

"That's about the size of it," Matt acknowledged.

"Four hundred pounds of flour. Joe, we got four hundred pounds of wheat flour left?"

The big redheaded clerk looked up from the pad where

114

he was scribbling furiously, and nodded. The storekeeper went down the list, totaled it, and told Matt, "Sixty-three dollars."

"All right; this is cash, not vouchers."

The man nodded and went off into the stockroom. Matt turned and idly watched the other customers. Idly until he saw the woman standing, hands on hips, glaring directly at him.

She was a pretty young thing, or would have been, except for the anger that tautened the skin across her cheekbones and drew her generous mouth into a hard, straight line.

She had long dark hair braided in a single strand down her back, wore a divided green riding skirt and a man's calico shirt. Her Spanish-style hat hung down her back, and she had a woven quirt on her wrist.

Matt looked at her inquisitively, nodding slightly, and she stamped a foot, spun around, and walked out of there, her shoulders set, back rigid.

Matt shrugged and turned back to the counter. The storekeeper had returned and he advised Matt, "Might be easier to load up around back, as much as you're taking. If you want to settle up now, I'll give you the list. You can tick it off as they load. Anything short, just let me know—as you can see, I'm kind of busy now."

"Fine." Matt gave the man four double eagles and pocketed his change. He folded the receipt and put it in his shirt pocket. Nodding to Rafferty, he went out onto the boardwalk, where MacArthur stood smoking a cigarette, watching the horses. MacArthur pinched off the ember from the end of the cigarette and put the butt in his pocket; on his salary he couldn't afford to waste perfectly good tobacco. Matt motioned to him, and he followed the lieutenant around to the store's back door. A wiry kid in shirtsleeves was stacking their flour, sugar, and beans at the end of the dock.

Matt checked off the supplies as MacArthur and Rafferty loaded the pack animals.

"That's supposed to do it," the kid said finally, mopping his head with a red handkerchief.

"And it does," Matt told him. "Thanks."

The kid nodded and went in, closing the door behind him. Rafferty had the last sack of beans on his shoulder and MacArthur was already in the saddle when Kincaid looked up to see a big man with a silver star on his coat.

"Help you?" Matt asked. The deputy was staring at Matt as if he were some unusual beast.

"Marshal wants to see you," the man grumbled in a voice so low and guttural that Kincaid had to strain to understand him. It was a few moments before he realized that the deputy had only half his tongue—the rest having been bitten cleanly away.

"The marshal?"

"That's what I said, looey," the deputy said.

"Kincaid," Matt told him coolly. "All right." He glanced at Rafferty and MacArthur. "You two take the—"

"Marshal don't want none of you leaving town until you've talked to him," the deputy interrupted thickly.

Matt eyed the deputy coldly, not liking his tone, but he nodded agreement. "All right. Which way?"

"Come on." Apparently the man felt obligated to escort them. He walked onto the main street, his shoulders rolling. He ignored the fighting in the street, the horse running free, its saddle inverted, and led them midway up the street to a low, dark building with a sagging roof and a small, weather-flaked sign that said "Town Marshal."

Matt swung down and tied his bay next to the appaloosa that stood there, its head bowed. Rafferty stepped up onto the boardwalk next to Kincaid and the deputy, who, at close range, smelled as if he hadn't taken a bath since getting out of diapers.

"Don't need you, Private," the deputy said, holding out a restraining hand. He managed to make *private* sound even more foul than *looey*.

"Stick with the horses, Rafferty. I'll be right out."

The deputy's eyes narrowed as if that might not be the case. Then he turned, twisted the loose-fitting brass door-knob, and opened the door to the marshal's office.

Inside, a fire burned in a Franklin stove. The marshal sat behind his cluttered desk in the corner of a cluttered office. A broad-shouldered, scarred man in a gray uniform stood near the rough plank door that led into a small jail cell. Beside him stood that spitfire of a girl.

Matt's eyebrows lifted in mild surprise and he walked to where the marshal sat, his feet propped up. Slovenly, narrow-eyed, the marshal of Gatlin wore a torn tweed jacket, a shirt with two buttons missing, baggy homespun pants, and a Colt revolver, which was pushed around to the front, dangling below his ample belly.

"Lieutenant." The marshal nodded as if it were a labor to do so. "Marshal Studdard."

"Marshal." Matt nodded, offered no hand, as none was offered him, and glanced at the woman in the corner. She looked as angry as before. It took a moment for the uniform worn by the man with her to come into focus. Then Matt knew it for what it was—a made-over Confederate uniform with some special militia insignia on the epaulettes.

The man wearing it was every bit as rigid as the girl; his face was badly scarred and his hair was snow white and carefully groomed, but for a bald spot the size of a silver dollar near the right ear, which seemed to be the result of a wound rather than time's affliction.

No one had said a word. Matt had to ask, "Is there something I can do for you all?"

"There damn sure is, but you wouldn't do it," the girl flared up. Matt didn't think it wise to ask her to be more specific.

He studied her with close interest. She was a fine-looking woman with full, high breasts and compelling hips. She caught his eyes on her and amazingly she flushed, deepening the crimson of anger that already colored her cheeks.

"Colonel Chadwick here," the marshal drawled, picking his teeth at the same time, "has a complaint against you. Wants me to restrain and reprimand you." The marshal said all of that in a perfect monotone, as if reading it clumsily from a sheet of paper on his desk.

"A complaint?" Matt repeated.

"Dammit, sir!" Chadwick sputtered. "Don't play the innocent Yankee. You know damned well what I mean!"

Matt thought momentarily of advising him that it was illegal to wear that Confederate uniform, but decided against it. He waited silently for the man to go on.

"The colonel wants—"

"I'll do my own talking," Chadwick interrupted, "since you seem loath to perform your duties, Marshal Studdard."

"I'm *loath* to do nothing, sir. But I don't quite have a handle on what exactly you expect me to do."

"I expect you by God to get those thieving, bastard Cheyenne off of Six-Bar, by force if necessary." The colonel stood before the wall lantern, hands clasped behind his back. The light fell on the bogus insignia on his shoulder. "Or have you forgotten where the money that holds this fleabag town together and provides your featherbed job comes from?"

"I haven't forgotten," the marshal said with monumental unconcern.

The colonel went on. "Before we drove up from Texas— Six-Bar and Chicken House, that is—there was no town here, and by God there won't be one again! It's only here now by the grace of Six-Bar, which has informed the railroad it prefers to ship from the vicinity of Gatlin."

Colonel Chadwick had a way of saying Six-Bar that made it sound holy, all-powerful, and entirely his own, which it apparently was. The marshal sighed, drummed his fingers on the desk, and looked to Kincaid.

"Where are you camped?"

"Five miles west," Matt told him.

"That's out of town limits, Colonel, and you know it. What the hell am I supposed to do?"

"Your duty."

"I do my job," the marshal said, showing mild irritation now, "*where* I'm supposed to do it. Until Gatlin extends its city limits out onto the plains, I've got no business out there. The sheriff—"

"The sheriff's in Oakley!"

Where he belongs, the marshal obviously thought, but he said nothing aloud.

"Am I missing something?" Matt Kincaid said abruptly. He was speaking to the colonel, but looking at the girl beside him. "I am transporting federal charges to a government reservation in Oklahoma. The marshal has nothing to say about that. Nor would the county sheriff if he was here. Nor do you, Colonel, although we have only one army in this country, and you are not a a member of it. You have nothing to say about it. You are impeding my job even now. I can't believe you contemplate anything else."

"By God, sir, you are impudent!" the colonel actually tottered, his body strung tight with rage. "A damn Yankee lieutenant!" he scoffed. "You are on my land, boy, scaring tallow off my steers, stealing steers—don't deny it—and robbing my cowhands."

"Now just a minute—" Matt protested.

"You wait a damned minute, boy!" Matt heard the door open behind him, but he did not turn just then. The colonel continued his diatribe. "I won't have it. You and your men allowing these damned Cheyenne to pillage their way south—"

"Now just hold it a damned minute, Colonel!" Matt exploded. "Just who owns that land out there?"

"Six-Bar."

"Title. You hold title?"

The colonel sputtered. "We've been grazing that land for six years, ever since—"

"I know, since you and Chicken House brought prosperity to Gatlin." The marshal seemed to smile a little at that. "What you're saying, without putting it in so many words, is that the land we're camped on is open range!"

"Six-Bar range!" Chadwick shouted illogically.

"You're missin' the point, Lieutenant."

This was a new voice, and Matt turned now toward the door. A tough-looking cowboy in a black silk shirt, wearing a silver-decorated vest and sleeve garters, lounged there.

"The point?" Matt said stiffly.

"Yeah, that's right." The man came erect. Matt noticed he wore his businesslike-looking Colt holstered low. There was an insolent curl to his lips. "The point is, the colonel wants you off. You get off or we move you."

"You, I suppose, are one of the movers?"

"That's right, Lieutenant." The man spat on the floor; he had a Deep South accent and was carrying an ax to grind that was so big you could almost see it.

"That's enough, Jacklin," the colonel said.

The gunman shrugged casually and leaned his shoulder against the wall, still glowering at Matt Kincaid.

"I've got forty men under me, Lieutenant," the colonel said, coming forward. His cheek twitched with some undefined emotion.

"Colonel—" the marshal tried to intervene, not liking the sound of this. He had seen range wars and didn't like them. What he liked even less was having the army scrap with Six-Bar. That *would* be the death of Gatlin.

"Shut up, Studdard," Chadwick said with contempt.

"I'm beginning to think you're a little mad, Colonel," Matt said. Jacklin twitched at that, but Matt went on recklessly: "You couldn't beat the army during the War, and you damned sure won't win with forty drunken cowboys."

"Won't I? Don't think I don't know how many men you have at your disposal, sir."

"And how many the *army* has at its disposal? As soon as reinforcements—"

"They would never get here, sir." Chadwick's voice was cold, flat. Kincaid had the sinking feeling that he was all too correct about the colonel's madness. "There would be no way to get word to the army. All of your men will be killed, I promise you. And buried so that no one ever knows of this."

"The marshal—" Matt began.

"The marshal is my man," Chadwick said stiffly. Studdard looked ashamedly away. "Believe me, it will happen that way."

120

"But why?"

"Why!" Chadwick laughed out loud. "Because I don't like you, Lieutenant Kincaid, don't like what that uniform stands for." His voice dropped and his eyes glittered in the dim light. "My home was burned during the War. My wife was killed—Jenny's mother. Yankees did it. Needlessly, brutally. When I moved to Texas, I married again. A young wife. Trailing north, we were hit by the Cheyenne. You know what they can do to a woman, Kincaid..." His voice was breaking badly now.

"Sir," Matt said as calmly as possible, "all of that is over."

"For whom! For the victors. The rapists, the murderers who went home. But not finished for me, sir, not for me. There's a pattern to this, you see." His voice was distant. "And it's started up again. Steers butchered, men robbed. Next comes the slaughter, the rape—" he glanced at his daughter.

Insane, Kincaid thought, and cursed his luck. Speaking with deliberate softness he asked, "You keep speaking of crimes my Cheyenne have committed. What crimes? What robbery? What thefts?"

"I think you know damned well," the colonel said slyly. "We're watching your camp, you know. I saw someone burying this." He nudged a blanket on the floor and, with his toe, revealed a fresh hide. Matt simply stared. He couldn't deny that it was Six-Bar, nor that his Cheyenne had taken it.

"Two young men. Their own people punished them," Kincaid said, glancing at the marshal, who was offering no help.

"And these," Chadwick said, triumphantly emptying his pockets. A gold watch glittered on the sheriff's desk, beside it a pocket knife, a photograph of a young woman, a walnut-handled razor.

"Where did these things come from?" Kincaid asked.

"From him." Chadwick swung the door to the jail cell open and Matt saw him on the floor. It was Lone Pine, beaten and bleeding, his face torn open as if he had been dragged. The gunman, Jacklin, was smiling insufferably. The marshal glanced at Kincaid.

"Seems like you've got 'em on a pretty loose rein," Studdard commented.

"What the hell have you done to the man?" Matt shouted. He entered the darkened cell and crouched beside Lone Pine, feeling his pulse, which was weak and erratic. "I'm taking this man with me," Matt announced, and his hand rested near his holster as he said it.

"Take him." Chadwick waved a hand. "Take him along with you. We'll find him again. We'll find you again, Kincaid. And when we do, you will meet the Wrath of God, sir! The Wrath of God!" His voice lowered. "His will be done."

There was nothing to say, absolutely nothing. Matt got Lone Pine to a sitting position and shouldered him. He walked toward the door, past the grinning, brutal face of Jacklin.

Outside, MacArthur and Rafferty glanced up expectantly, their expressions shifting rapidly as they saw the beaten Cheyenne.

"Who is it?"

"Lone Pine. The son of a bitch had to sneak off and get pretties to show his woman." Matt threw him over one of the pack animals and tied him on.

Chadwick had come onto the boardwalk with Jacklin siding him and the girl, Jenny, just behind. Rafferty asked in a low voice, "Who is that, sir?"

"That is the Wrath of God, Private. The Wrath of God."

He explained the rest of it as they rode out toward the camp. Rafferty shook his head and muttered, "Another John Allan Huggins, huh?"

"No." Matt was thoughtful. "Not another Huggins. I wish he were."

"He'll fight, sir?" MacArthur asked.

"He'll fight," Matt answered grimly.

ten _____

"We must smoke."

"We've already smoked." Pop Evans looked impatiently at his watch, saw that it was too late to return to Outpost Number Nine tonight, put the watch away, and sighed heavily, looking again at Jake Ten Knives, who sat on the blanket inside his tipi and slowly, carefully stuffed a clay pipe with a blend of willowbark and tobacco.

"Can't we come to the point?"

Jake Ten Knives wagged a finger at Evans. "You see, it is no wonder you have no license to trade with the Cheyenne. The White Father knows that you do not keep the Cheyenne customs. He knows that you will not smoke and exchange gifts, ask after Jake's children, speak of the weather and the buffalo."

"Dammit, Jake! Cohen said you were in a hurry to get rid of those furs."

"Sometimes Jake in a hurry, sometimes not in a hurry." He passed the pipe to Pop. "But we must smoke, we must follow the customs of my people. You are lucky it is old Jake you trade with—many Cheyenne would be very offended. Many Cheyenne would take your hair for your rudeness."

Jake himself held a knife in his hands, and Pop Evans swallowed hard, inhaling the tobacco smoke, watching Jake's unsmiling face.

"When am I going to get to see those furs?" Pop asked.

"It is too dark to see the furs now, isn't it so, Evans?" Jake asked, waving an unconcerned hand.

"Now!" Pop felt dizzy from the smoke, from the closeness of the tipi. "Yes, it is too late."

"So tomorrow we will look. Tomorrow you will see, fine furs, plenty of money for you, Evans. Poor Jake gets very little from this." He shook his head with a sadness that hardly touched Pop's heart. He had been sitting there most of the afternoon while Jake delayed first one way and then another; if this was typical of the Indian traders, he wondered how they had ever gotten their reputation for shrewdness.

"Tomorrow," Pop said wearily. There would be a bed for him at the agency offices, at least. Then tomorrow the deal could be consummated. He would lose only half a day's profits from his store if he closed the deal quickly.

And what was half a day's profit more? They were talking about five thousand. Now that he thought of it, why cut Sergeant Cohen in at all? There was no way Cohen could force him. . . . With that thought warming him, Pop bid his goodnight to Jake Ten Knives and strode whistling toward the agency building.

"Sh!" Cohen's whisper was loud in the total darkness. McBride came to an utter standstill, waiting while the shadow on the small windowpane passed.

"All right."

Reb crept forward, the bundle of trousers in his hands. He had six canteens around his neck, and they banged together as he stumbled.

"Chrissakes, McBride!" Cohen hissed.

"Sorry, sorry."

Cohen was at the door now. It was dark all across the camp. He waved to the gate guard, got a wave in response, and Cohen nodded his head.

"Come on."

McBride crept forward, followed by Trueblood, who was

draped with boots. Cohen moved stealthily out onto the boardwalk and muttered, "Turning into a burglar at my age."

"Maybe we ought to put the stuff back," Trueblood said nervously.

"I'll be damned," Ben said. "We're passing that inspection one way or the other. Come on." He scuttled across the parade like a cloud shadow, McBride and Trueblood at his heels.

The barracks door seemed half a mile away, but they made it, Trueblood stumbling over the threshold, sending boots flying.

"For Christ's sake," Corporal Miller said.

"Shut up. Black them windows out," Cohen ordered.

Blankets were hung over the windows, and Cohen had a lamp lit. Then he methodically walked among the soldiers, exchanging their worn equipment for new.

"Don't lose anything, don't put a wrinkle in them pants," he warned them. "It's all got to go back."

He nearly stumbled over a pair of beautifully shined boots. "Who owns these?" he demanded.

"They're mine," McBride said.

"Well, Christ, McBride, put 'em away."

"I want to exchange them."

"Why?" Cohen looked at the glossy boots, mystified.

"Look closer, Sarge."

"Closer?" Cohen did so. "Jesus, what is that?"

"They just wouldn't take a shine. I dipped them in gelatine in Rothausen's kitchen, but it's coming off," McBride said. "I'll take a pair of size nine."

"You'll wear size six tomorrow," Cohen said, handing him the boots.

"Jesus, Sarge!"

"For one day, McBride. You can make it one day, can't you?"

McBride hesitated and Cohen said, "Sixes or twelves— that's all I've got."

"Give the fuckin' twelves to me. I'll wear eight pairs of socks. Then the inspector won't have to count the holes in *them*."

Cohen tossed him the boots and McBride, sighing, slipped into them. Trueblood was wrapping the used gear and worn clothing in a blanket in the center of the room. Miller stood with his back to the door, leaning against it, his eyes furtive.

"What if Evans gets back tonight, Sarge?" Miller asked dismally. "Jesus, we'll all be hung."

"He won't be back. I'm paying Jake Ten Knives a dollar an hour to hold him on the agency. For that kind of money, Jake'll hogtie him and sit on him if he tries to get away before the inspection is over."

He sat on the log, running a whetstone along the edge of his saber. Mandalian's shadow fell across him and John Fairchild whirled around, his eyes wide.

"Just me," Windy said. He had a cup of coffee in his hand and his rifle over the crook of his arm. He stared out across the dark and empty land, watching as a screech owl winged past over the dark river, cutting a darting shadow.

"What do you want, Mr. Mandalian?" Fairchild asked with a strained patience.

"Nothin'." Windy shrugged. "Just movin' around a bit. Thought maybe you'd want to talk, discuss this patrol."

"Nothing's happened, what is there to discuss?"

"Nothin' much if you look at it that way." The scout wanted to ease into a conversation with this young officer, to instruct him without seeming to, but John Fairchild had closed all the doors. What did he think he was going to do with that saber anyway? It was good for slicing melons, Windy supposed. He stood there awhile longer, watching the impatience gnaw away at Fairchild.

"Evenin', sir," Windy said. He nodded his head and walked back across the camp, listening to the whispery sound of stone against steel.

Olsen was still up, poking at the fire with a burned stick.

Windy walked up beside the NCO and stood silently watching the embers as Gus stirred them up. The night was remarkably warm, with hardly a breeze. Stars lay scattered brilliantly across a limitless expanse of black sky.

"Having a talk with the young lieutenant, were you?" Gus asked without glancing up.

"It didn't work out."

"Tell me about it," Olsen muttered.

"Tell you what, Gus, this scares me. Purely scares me." Windy crouched down and Gus turned toward him with surprise. That was quite an admission for Windy, though it was probably exaggeration.

"How's that?"

"I've ridden under green officers before. Some of 'em so green they were sprouting here and there. But this one's different. When the ignorant are cocksure," Windy said with a slow wink, "you've got trouble."

Olsen shrugged. "Likely we won't even make hostile contact."

"Likely." Windy rose and stretched, nodding good night, "But if we do, we got us a problem, I'm afraid. The kid wants heroics, Gus, he wants blood and guts, powder and smoke, and that worries me. That surely does worry me."

The sensible thing to do was to rise and march, but the Cheyenne had just finished an all-night march. There was no way on earth they could be roused again so soon.

And so Kincaid simply ordered the guard doubled, passed the word to his own troops, and prayed. The Wrath of God was out there somewhere, and he was ready to come a-killin'.

"He just can't be that crazy," Wojensky commented in disbelief. "To take on the army—he's just cutting his own throat."

"He doesn't care, Corporal. That's the point. He's one of the kind who just doesn't care if it's his own blood that's spilled, just so there's blood."

"But he'll need an army that feels the same way, won't

he? Has he got forty crazy men behind him?"

"He's got forty men who ride for the Six-Bar brand. Men who likely have fought Comanches, Mexican raiders, rustlers, and hard weather together. Most of them will be ex-Confederate soldiers, Wojensky. They've seen fighting, they don't like the color blue or the word 'Indian.' And they've got better weapons than we do. I know that; they know it."

"Join the army for adventure," Wojensky said with a touch of bitterness. "Confusing, isn't it? We've somehow gotten ourselves into a position where we're protecting the people we *were* protecting the people *against*."

Malone appeared at the flap of Kincaid's tent, his rifle gripped tightly in his fist. "Someone's approaching camp from the east, sir."

Kincaid belted on his sidearm and grabbed his hat. Following Malone out into the night, he looked across the darkened plains, seeing nothing yet. But there was dust on the light breeze, the clopping of hooves.

"One rider," Wojensky said after a minute.

And it was. The horse, a leggy appaloosa, appeared suddenly, a white shadow against the black earth, and as the rider swung down, Matt let his hand slide off the butt of his Schofield revolver.

"Miss Chadwick." He touched the brim of his hat to her in greeting.

Jenny Chadwick walked to within two paces of the lieutenant. Her hair was loose down her back, her eyes sparkling as she looked up at the tall officer. Her breasts rose and fell with the deep breaths she took.

"I have to talk to you."

"All right." Kincaid nodded to Wojensky and Malone, and they lost themselves in the darkness. "In my tent?"

"Here, if it's all right."

"It is." There was a softness in Jenny Chadwick's voice now that had not been there earlier, and an urgency.

He waited patiently for her to begin. When she did, her voice was agitated.

128

"The colonel held a meeting tonight, his men and all the citizens of Gatlin. There was free liquor—it makes the convincing simpler." Matt noted in passing that she called her own father "the colonel," and wondered about that.

She swallowed and went on. "At first I honestly thought he was just trying to bluff you, to protect his land and property."

It wasn't the colonel's land, but Matt let that go by. "And now?"

"He's deadly serious. It's an idea that just popped up, I think, this thought of a massacre. But it was born and it grew. It's a monstrous thing now, this idea, and it's unstoppable. They will come, Lieutenant, they will. All their hatreds—of the army, the North, the Cheyenne—have found a scapegoat in you."

"I appreciate your coming to me," Matt said quietly, "but I took your father seriously all along."

"He must have eighty men!" Jenny said. "I came to ask you to leave."

"I can't."

"You can. You could slip away. Leave the Cheyenne here. No one could blame you."

Matt smiled grimly at that. Who else could be blamed? He supposed the girl saw this mission as a noble gesture. Warn the soldiers, and to hell with the Cheyenne.

"Your father will become a wanted man, a murderer, Miss Chadwick. He will never, never get away with this. You are wasting your arguments on me. I would advise you to try talking to your father. Perhaps the colonel's mind can still be changed."

"It can't. You don't know him. Do you want to see your men die?"

"Do you think I do?"

"No . . . but then"—she was genuinely confused— "why won't you leave?"

"Besides the fact that it is not in the army's tradition to run from mob threats? Besides duty and honor? I do not think I could explain it to you if you don't understand, Miss

Chadwick. There are women in that camp, and children who, believe me, have never lifted any scalps. Do you know what will happen to them if your father carries out this insane plan?"

Jenny covered her face. Matt tore her hands away. "Talk to your father. Talk to the townspeople, the cowboys. Convince them that this is a terible and costly game they are playing. Failing that, Jenny, ride away as quickly as you can. You will not want to witness what happens tomorrow."

She staggered back toward her horse, her face ashen, and Kincaid watched her go. A decision had been rattling around in Kincaid's mind, one that was difficult to make and to justify, but one that Jenny Chadwick's information had solidified. Kincaid found Wojensky at the supply dump, handling out extra ammunition to the soldiers in anticipation of a dawn attack.

"Sir." Wojensky rose and saluted.

Briefly, Kincaid told him what he wanted, and he wanted it before first light. "We'll fight dismounted, Wo. Two files facing east. The Republican will be on our unprotected right flank, and the reserves will form the left flank."

Kincaid sketched a rough L in the dirt. Easy Company's soldiers were represented by two lines at the base of the L, facing eastward, toward Gatlin. Wojensky was wrestling with Kincaid's statement. Did he mean . . . ?

"Did I understand the lieutenant to say the *reserves* would form the northern flank?"

"You did. Arm the Cheyenne, Wojensky. By God, we need them now. Have Dancing Horse report to me."

"Sir, the orders—" Wojensky fell silent. Kincaid needed no reminding what the orders were. "Right away, sir." He saluted and designated Rafferty to continue handing out extra cartridges.

"Malone!" the corporal called on his way to Dancing Horse's tipi. "Get the Cheyenne weapons. Start rousing the warriors."

Malone stared for a minute, then shrugged and got to it.

The sky was paling already, and after a few striding steps, Malone broke into a run.

Matt Kincaid had returned to his tent. Carefully he shaved and then packed his kit away. He cleaned and oiled his revolver and walked again to the flap of his tent. The Cheyenne were scurrying from their tipis. An occasional war cry creased the predawn silence. There was nothing left to do. Nothing but hope that the Wrath of God had somehow been subdued, that he would not come, that blood would not stain the long grass. But it was a slender hope.

With a start, Matt realized that the eastern sky had taken on a pale rose hue. He tugged his hat lower and went out into the bleak morning.

The gates swung open at dawn, and the three soldiers entered Outpost Number Nine. Two were enlisted men, bewhiskered and trail-weary. The third wore the gold oak leaves of a major.

The officer sat rigidly in the saddle. His face was extremely narrow, his nose overambitious, his eyes small and closely set. This combination of features, along with his predatory reputation, had earned the major a distinctive nickname.

"God, it's Hawk MacCauley," Corporal Wilson said.

McBride lifted himself from his bunk and walked to the door. Regiment had indeed sent Major Peter "Hawk" MacCauley to inspect Outpost Number Nine. This was something to turn even the redoubtable heart of Sergeant Cohen to rapid palpitation.

"Wonder if Cohen knows."

"He will shortly."

"What?" Kip Schoendienst looked up feebly. For the last week he had been expecting the executioner's ax to fall. His nerves were completely shot. He stood at McBride's shoulder, gawking at the sharp-faced major who was dismounting in front of headquarters, and asked, "Is that . . . ?"

"Nothing to do with you," McBride said reassuringly.

131

He attempted a smile, but it didn't work. Schoendienst slunk away.

"The captain can't delay the court-martial any longer, can he? I mean, when the inspection's over, Hawk MacCauley will ride back to Regiment. He'll have to carry a report to the TJA."

"That's about the size of it," Miller told him.

"The poor son of a bitch."

Reb looked toward Schoendienst's bunk. The kid was dressing now, in his borrowed uniform. Pop Evans's crisp new clothes did nothing to make Schoendienst look any sharper. He looked like a scarecrow newly decked out. And much of the straw was leaking out.

Miller slapped Reb on the shoulder. "Let's get with it. No sense in us getting on Cohen's permanent shit list."

Dawn was breaking clear. The sun was warming, but the day promised to be far from bright. It was a dismal dawning and a bloody one.

Windy's arm rose in the air, his rifle clenched in his hand. He was silhouetted against the coming sun, and seemed a dark omen.

Olsen felt his heart skip a beat, and he glanced automatically at Fairchild, who rode with his eyes turned down to the night-frosted grass.

"Hostile contact, sir," Olsen whispered. Fairchild's head came up sharply, his eyes suddenly bright. Olsen nodded toward Windy, who sat his mount atop the low knoll, his rifle still raised.

Fairchild lifted his white gelding into a canter and Olsen urged his own horse to keep stride. The scout had dismounted by the time they reached him, and had eased back some from the skyline.

"Where?" Fairchild demanded, dismounting while his horse was still in motion. His face was flushed. His left hand unconsciously gripped the handle of his saber.

"In the oaks, sir." Windy lifted a gnarled finger. "You

132

can't see 'em, but I smell woodsmoke, heard a horse nicker. They're down there, all right."

Fairchild frowned in disgust. He studied the stand of oaks through his field glasses, seeing nothing. "I don't see what in hell—"

The muffled report of a rifle cut through the lieutenant's disbelief. A puff of smoke rose from the oaks, and the white horse danced away crazily, biting at its flank, where a long streak of crimson had appeared. The three men hit the ground and John Fairchild's face was utterly pale, a curious mixture of anger, disbelief, frustration, and—most definitely—cold fear.

eleven ─────────

The sun was in his eyes, and the perspiration that trickled down his forehead stung them. It was warm, but there was a cooling breeze. Nevertheless, John Fairchild's shirt was plastered to his chest and back, stuck to his hide with cold sweat.

An occasional shot racketed over the prairie as the renegades potted at them from the oaks. Windy was beside Fairchild, chewing on a wad of tobacco, his piercing eyes squinting into the sun, awaiting the lieutenant's orders.

Waiting.

They were all waiting for him, and his mind had gone blank and fuzzy. Tactics, determination, half-baked concepts of heroism—all had flown clean out of his skull with the first shot that had darted across the empty space between them and torn a gash in the flank of the white gelding.

"Sir?" Olsen was at his side. "Sir? How do you want to proceed?"

"What?" He did not turn his head. How to proceed? God, how was he supposed to know? Charge them, kill them all, run? Hope they would withdraw? He swallowed his pride.

"What do you recommend, Sergeant?"

"Put a few volleys over their heads, sir. Let them know we mean business. They might surrender without a fight."

"Mandalian?" Fairchild asked. He twisted his head toward the scout, keeping it as close to the ground as possible.

Fairchild's hat had fallen off, but he didn't bother to pick it up.

"I'll ride with Olsen's idea. Can't hurt, and it won't cost us more'n a few rounds."

"All right." Fairchild nodded, and then the empty realization came to him that he couldn't even recall exactly how to order this done. He cursed himself silently, and told Gus Olsen, "Have a few rounds put into the trees. Fire high."

"Yes, sir."

Olsen slipped back from the rim and passed the word to the entrenched troopers. Fairchild heard the sounds of rifles being cocked. From the corner of his eye he watched as Olsen raised his arm and lowered it.

The volley was louder than Fairchild had expected; his ears rang. A thick cloud of black smoke rolled across the knoll. He kept his head buried in his arms, knowing Windy was watching him.

"Load! Fire!" he heard Olsen's confident voice shout, and again the rifles exploded, again the acrid smoke stung his eyes and nose.

"Load! Fire!"

Again, the thunder of the guns echoed through Fairchild's head, and he wanted to scream at them, make them stop it, but he didn't dare. He knew his voice would tremble and squeak.

Olsen fired three more volleys, and then the prairie fell deathly silent.

Fairchild heard the hooves of a running horse behind him, and his head snapped around. He was clawing for his pistol when he recognized the rider. It was Windy's Delaware friend, Joseph Hatchet.

The scout swung down and walked to Windy to report. Windy paid them, so they reported to him, not to the army. But it caused a slow anger to rise in Fairchild.

It was easier to be angry when the shots died down, he discovered. Now he saw the Delaware and his scout in close conversation, and he was aware of Gus Olsen's eyes on him. The soldiers had maintained their positions along the knoll, but to Fairchild it seemed they were all staring at him, wondering at his indecision.

Probably only five minutes had passed since Windy had spotted the renegades in the oaks, but it seemed like five hours to Fairchild. He forced himself to rise, to find his hat, forced himself to swagger among the men.

To hell with them, he thought. He would have them all up before Conway when they got back. He knew what they were thinking—they thought him a coward.

The saber at his side seemed ridiculous now, heavy and awkward. With difficulty he made it to where Windy and Hatchet stood talking.

"What's happening, Mandalian?"

"Hatchet had him a closer look-see, sir. Seems they ain't our young Cheyenne. They're Arapaho."

"Arapaho?"

"Yes, sir. But that ain't a problem."

"They want a good fight," Hatchet explained, his bronzed hands making tiny chopping motions. "We shoot at them, they shoot at us. No one get hurt, everyone go home with honor."

Fairchild snorted with amazement. "Good fight! What kind of joke is this?"

"No joke, sir. Happens all the time," Windy said. "They get to fire their guns, brag back at their lodges."

"And we indulge this play!"

"It beats a killin' fight," Windy reminded him.

"How do we know what they want!" Fairchild shouted. He realized his voice was loud enough to be heard by all the men, so he forced himself to breathe deeply, to quiet down. "These men have attacked the United States Army. How do we know they want to play at fighting?"

"I know," Hatchet said. "It is the way."

"I'm with Hatchet, sir. If they wanted to ambush us, we'd never have come up on them like this."

"And your advice is?"

"Play the game, sir," Windy said, spitting.

Fairchild was beside himself with rage.

136

"This patrol is not going to be fired upon and treat it as a game, an amusing incident, something to brag to Captain Conway about."

"Sir," Gus Olsen tried to intervene, "Windy and Hatchet are right. This is not war. It's a quirk we have to deal with. In the old days, maybe they would have tried to take our scalps. Now they confine themselves to shooting over our heads and drifting off when they're finished. Let them have it their way, sir."

"*That* is your recommendation, is it, Sergeant Olsen?" Fairchild rocked on his heels, his eyes sliding from one face to the next. Gus Olsen didn't like the look in those eyes. The man had been scared, and now he was trying to prove he wasn't. There was a good chance he would rack up casualties where there need be none.

"I was right about you, Olsen." He leveled a trembling finger. "I told Captain Conway about you and he scoffed. He took your side. If he could see you now, I wonder what he would say. And don't think he won't find out! "God, I'm surrounded by cowards. Surrounded." He whirled around to face the patrol. "Mount! By God, we're going after those bastards."

"Sir!" Olsen's face was etched with anxiety, and Fairchild, reading it as fear, laughed.

"Remain if you like, Sergeant. Don't worry—I won't make you risk your cowardly skin. Mount, dammit!" he repeated to the soldiers, who stood watching with vacant expressions. Fairchild was obviously out of control now.

"That's an order! I'll have you all court-martialed!"

Slowly they mounted, looking helplessly to Olsen, who could do nothing but follow Fairchild to his horse, pleading with him.

"It's not necessary, sir."

"By God, they've attacked!"

Fairchild gathered the reins of his white horse, not sparing a glance at the wound, which was deeper than Olsen had first guessed.

"Sir." Olsen put his hand on Fairchild's bridle. "Please

listen to the scouts, they know what they're talking about."

"Get your hand off that bridle, Sergeant."

"Sir—"

"I said *off!* That's an order, Sergeant Olsen! You *do* know what an order is, don't you?"

Fairchild whipped out his saber, and Olsen fell back three paces. Looking at Windy, he saw that the scout hadn't moved either. A mournful-looking Joseph Hatchet sided the white scout.

"At a walk!" Fairchild hollered to his men, and started his own horse forward.

"Sarge!" Private Armstrong looked to Olsen for direction, but Gus didn't respond. He would do the kid no favor by telling him to disobey a direct order in the face of the enemy. He turned his head.

Fairchild had his riders at the crown of the hill now, and he lifted his saber high. The sun glinted off the polished steel. Olsen saw that, and then he saw the Arapaho. Standing in the path of the horses, a lone Indian danced and chanted, waving his gun.

"Charge!" Fairchild shouted, and spurred his horse savagely. The Arapaho who had been sporting around to prove his nerve to the others now stood frozen, eyes wide. Fairchild, a good twenty yards in front of his reluctant force, was riding down hard on the bare-chested Arapaho.

Olsen tried to shout but could not; he knew it would make no difference anyway. In the next seconds he saw death unfold, battle-time slowing the sequence incredibly so that Olsen was aware of each inevitable motion.

The sun flashed on Fairchild's saber, and the Arapaho's mouth opened in a soundless expression of fear. He went to his knee, lifting the rifle stock to his shoulder as Fairchild looked back, urging on his laggard patrol.

Olsen saw Windy rushing up behind Fairchild, saw Hatchet get to one knee, saw Fairchild's mouth open as if to shout a command, and then the smoke billowed from the muzzle of the Arapaho's rifle.

Fairchild jerked, and only then did the roar of the rifle

reach Olsen's ears. The lieutenant hunched forward and then twisted back. The saber fell against the grass, and crimson smeared Fairchild's tunic.

Olsen flinched reflexively as Hatchet fired beside him and the Arapaho who had been scrambling toward the cover of the oaks fell in a heap, Hatchet's bullet through his heart.

The charging patrol slowed at once. There was no enemy, no officer. From the other side of the oaks the Arapaho took to the plains, riding low over their horses, only flashes of color and patches of shadow at this distance.

Olsen stood, fired his rifle into the air, and shouted frantically. Windy fired as well, and they waved their arms, halting the charge.

Then, slowly, they rode down onto the flats. Near the oaks, a crumpled figure lay sprawled. The Arapaho had died instantly. His rifle was flung some distance away.

Olsen stepped down and led his horse to where the body of John Fairchild, Jr. lay. The lieutenant had taken the bullet just under the collarbone. In all likelihood, his heart had stopped before he hit the ground.

Nevertheless, Gus got down beside him and took a stab at trying to find a pulse in Fairchild's throat. There was none. He glanced up, muttering a series of slow, deeply felt curses.

Windy was watching, his eyes unreadable. He held the saber in his hand, and now he handed it to Olsen, who took it and turned it over, feeling the sharp edge, noticing the scrollwork on the guard and blade. He looked again at the scout, but there was little enough to say.

Bending down, Gus picked up the young officer and slung him across his shoulder, with Hatchet's help they got him across the saddle of that fancy white warhorse.

They came with the dawn. An army of rabble, of malcontents. They were no regular army, those who followed the Wrath of God out of the sun and onto the plains, but that made them no less dangerous—they all had guns.

There were at least sixty men, Kincaid guessed. They

came on horseback and afoot, riding in the Six-Bar chuck-wagon and on a freighter's rig. The cattle scattered as they came, their wide eyes astonished at the herd of men.

Kincaid glanced behind him to where his men stood in two staggered ranks, and then to the north, where he saw no one—just as he was supposed to be able to see no one.

And then he merely waited. Death was knocking at the door, and he was about to fling it wide and let it in.

twelve _____

The Wrath of God was there in the forefront, but he made no move to break free, to come forward and talk. There was to be no speaking, only war.

Kincaid watched him ride before his legions. A tall, narrow man wearing an immaculate, spurious uniform. What forces of evil did he think he was riding against?

Townspeople and cowboys tramped along behind, shouting encouragement to each other. What was this to them? A holy war or perhaps mere entertainment, for God's sake!

Some of them were going to die, painfully, brutally, and yet they came marching, some grinning or laughing. At least, he noticed, Jenny Chadwick was not there to see this.

He glanced again at his men. They were ready. The order was to fire at will once the battle began, if it did begin. Kincaid would have asked them to shoot low, to try not to kill unless it was necessary, but he couldn't give that sort of order in battle, no matter how crazy the conflict seemed. To spare a man may be to be killed yourself.

He was aware suddenly of movement on the southern flank and, looking that way, he saw a herd of three hundred or so steers being pushed between the two forces.

"They're going to stampede them at us," Matt called to Wojensky.

Kincaid hesitated. He pondered having his men fire a

141

volley, perhaps stampeding the steers back the other way, in the direction of Chadwick's own army. Yet he still hoped actual gunfire might somehow be averted. Kincaid had been in enough fights to know that the first shot would trigger a barrage of sympathetic fire.

In a few moments it all became academic.

From somewhere in the front of Chadwick's line, a rifle was touched off. Whether or not that was a signal, the cowboys hazing the cattle toward them drew their sixguns and began firing into the air, whooping at the steers, spurring them to motion.

The cattle came in a thundering rush, eyes wide, horns clacking together; clouds of dust billowed into the clear air.

A shout came up from Chadwick's "army," and they came rushing forward as the cattle separated the two forces and then swung toward Kincaid's position.

"Fire!" Matt shouted, dropping his hand, and Easy Company opened up.

Wojensky settled his sights on the blue shirt of a cowboy who was pushing the steers toward them, and fired. The man slapped at his shirt and fell from the saddle.

The herd had already been turned now, and it raced toward Kincaid's position. Over the sea of rolling cattle, Matt could see Chadwick's mob rushing eagerly toward them. He saw a blacksmith with a sledgehammer, another man with only a pitchfork, running and jumping like kids at a picnic.

From his prone position, Malone swung his Springfield toward the lead steer, held his breath, squeezed off, and saw the steer go down. Those behind it trampled over it, stumbled, or turned aside.

Malone shoveled in a fresh cartridge and took down another steer. That big .45-70 bullet had its disadvantages, but a cow was no match for it. Kincaid was shouting for his men to do just what Malone was already doing, but it was impossible to hear him above the rumble of the herd.

Wojensky got to his feet, shouting for those around him

to do the same, knowing they were less likely to be trampled if they were standing. Even a panicked, stampeding steer will try to turn aside for a man.

Wojensky fired twice, and saw a steer buckle at the knees and somersault. Then he felt a bullet whoosh past his ear. Standing up did have its disadvantages.

Angrily, Wojensky turned his rifle on the men behind the herd. He felt the recoil of his rifle, and saw the screen of smoke explode from the muzzle. As it cleared away, he saw a man down. Amazingly, six men around the wounded man had simply stopped cold, staring at their companion in disbelief.

Black smoke drifted across the prairie, mingling with the dust of the herd, obscuring all vision. Wojensky looked around, saw the cattle nearly on top of them, and shouted a futile warning.

Malone stood among the steers, firing methodically, not at the cattle now, for that was useless, but at the chuckwagon that had been tipped over by a panicked driver and was now being used as a barricade.

Some of the cattle had turned and were now running through Chadwick's army, scattering them. Kincaid saw a cowboy go down beneath their hooves. Looking along his own ranks, he saw a blue uniform flattened against the ground, and cursed.

Malone was a rock standing above a sea of rolling, lurching brown steers. Amazingly he had not been touched, although hundreds of cattle streamed past him, dividing where he stood to merge again afterward. He fired with mechanical precision, loading, firing, loading.

Kincaid tried to locate Chadwick, but could not, and fired his revolver in the direction of a charging man. There were few enough of them charging now. Some of their number had been hit, and that had halted them in their tracks.

Beyond the chuckwagon, which had spilled its contents over the prairie, Kincaid could already see some of the townspeople fleeing the battlefield. Apparently no one had told them that bullets sting.

Chadwick's cowboys were a different story. This was a range war, and they had seen a few of those. He turned to his right and returned the fire of a cowboy on a buckskin horse, and then felt a tug at his collar as if someone had grabbed him.

No one had; it was a bullet near enough to rip a smoldering hole in his collar. Kincaid went down on a knee and spun back.

He had a glimpse only of the cruel face of Jacklin before the black smoke from the muzzle of Jacklin's pistol veiled the space between them.

Kincaid fired back, shoved his way through the slowing, milling cattle, and ducked low, working toward Jacklin. He lifted his head from behind a steer's back, and Jacklin fired again.

The steer bawled with pain and kicked out, and Kincaid moved, still in a crouch. He popped up again from out of the undulating sea of steers and fired at Jacklin. Missing, he fired again and he saw Jacklin go to the side of the sorrel he rode. Matt could not be sure whether he was hit or not.

He started moving toward Jacklin rapidly. The gunslick's sorrel lurched among the cattle, and Matt shoved at the steers, trying to get through.

He saw Jacklin's hand clinging to the pommel. That and his leg, clad in black jeans. Then he saw nothing else for a long while.

Malone had been firing steadily at the chuckwagon, keeping the men there pinned down. Again he settled his sights and fired. But this time a violent explosion followed the impact of his bullet.

The cook must have kept a can of powder in the wagon; either that, or explosives had been brought from town for use in the battle.

Pieces of planking, cans of tinned goods, hats, and rolls of wire were hurtled across the grass. Black smoke rose in a column thirty feet high. Those nearest the wagon were slammed to the earth by the force of the explosion. A man screamed, others ran.

Malone himself was knocked flat, though he was fifty yards off. He felt a wash of hot wind and was surprised to find himself seated on the ground among the bawling cattle.

A half-dozen horses ran free on the plains. Their riders limped after them or lay flat on the ground, moaning. The smoke had settled, and now it smothered Chadwick's army, obscuring it behind inky clouds.

Chadwick had fallen back, but he had his cowboys with him. Formed into a loose rank, they were ready to charge as soon as the drifting smoke cleared.

Kincaid could see nothing before him, but he could see the northern flank clearly. It was time to call in the reserves, and he lifted his arm, waving them down.

The air was suddenly filled with the war cries of charging Cheyenne.

They had painted their faces and their ponies for this battle, and they rode from out of the north as their ancestors had done in the Shining Times.

The smoke cleared and the cowboys found themselves in an unfortunate and deadly position. They had Easy Company before them and Cheyenne on the flank. The smart ones turned tail and rode, knowing they were suddenly outclassed if not outnumbered.

A few stayed to fight, but it was a short fight. Another cowboy went down, and the rest threw down their guns, their hands grabbing at the sky as Kincaid's men rushed forward to meet the charge of the Cheyenne.

Disappointment wreathed the faces of the Indians. The enemy had surrendered too easily. They had been primed for battle, and now they wanted it. Two Fingers rode his pony in a tight circle, goading the prisoners.

Kincaid shouted to Dancing Horse, reminding him of their agreement—no killing unless necessary. It could only turn out badly for the Cheyenne if whites were killed, no matter the circumstances.

Dancing Horse, wearing a feathered warbonnet, shouted

to his men and rode among them, congratulating and calming them.

It was only at that moment that Kincaid saw him.

The Wrath of God lay sprawled in the dry grass. His arms were pinned under him, his legs flung out unnaturally. When Kincaid rolled him over, he found that Chadwick's blood had stained the long grass red beneath his body.

Someone had gotten the colonel through the heart. A nice shot, expertly placed. Had it been one of Kincaid's own men or a Cheyenne?

"He's dead."

"It is good," Dancing Horse said. He sat his pony with the wind shifting the feathers of his bonnet. His face had been painted with yellow and blue. Just then, Dancing Horse looked as fierce and as proud as any Cheyenne on the wild plains.

It had been their last battle, and they had been victorious. They held their heads high with pride; there would be tales to tell around the campfire this night.

No one took credit or blame for killing Chadwick and Kincaid left it at that. They buried him on the plains with two of his cowboys.

It was difficult to rouse the proper feelings, but Matt Kincaid, hat in hands, said a few words over the man. Then he looked around him.

The Six-Bar cattle were scattered for miles across the plains. The burned chuckwagon still smoldered. Beside it, a cowboy sat holding his head, moaning horribly. Chadwick lay beneath the sod, and Gatlin was full of cowardly men who were now placing the blame on one another, fearful that the army might punish them, that they might lose the railhead.

Matt smiled. His men were weary, smoke-blackened, but they had stood, and would do so again, if necessary. Two Fingers stood next to Malone, still watching the grave, and behind those two, Iron Owl sat with a fiercely painted Cheyenne, discussing the battle as brave equals, not as master and slave.

The Cheyenne had lost the war for the plains, Matt reflected, but here, this morning, Dancing Horse's band had won a great battle.

Wojensky led his horse to him, and Matt put on his hat and stepped into the stirrups. He gave his orders to the corporal, and then said to Dancing Horse, "It's time to be moving. There is still a long trail to Oklahoma."

"Still a long trail," Dancing Horse agreed. His eyes sparkled now, and Matt smiled. They had come to understand each other, these two warriors. As strange as it seemed, Matt himself no longer looked forward to the end of this trail with eagerness, for, once there, something irreplaceable would be lost, something that could exist only on the plains among free men.

He glanced at Dancing Horse again, and there was sadness in the Cheyenne's eyes. He too knew it was the last battle, the last trail. He shouted to his men, sending them racing off across the grass, whooping and shouting. When they were gone, Dancing Horse turned his attention again to Kincaid and said only once, very softly, "Thank you."

And then he was gone, back among his people.

"What about them steers?" Malone asked. When Kincaid did not look at him, he repeated the question. "Sir? What about them dead steers? They'll rot out here, and we could use the meat."

"Leave them, Malone," Kincaid said quietly. The wind was in his hair, pressing his tunic to his chest. He looked around him at the empty range, the scattered dead cattle, and then again at the fresh grave of Colonel Chadwick. "Leave them for Chadwick."

Then he swung his horse's head around and rode rapidly back toward the camp, and Malone, hands on hips, sleeves rolled up, watched him go. Finally he shrugged and shouldered his rifle, holding it by the barrel, and started a long, ambling walk back to camp.

"Come on, Rafferty," he snapped. "Going to sit there all goddamned day?"

Rafferty glanced up in surprise, shrugged, and got to his

feet. Together they walked across the dry grass, the clean air whipping away the lingering scent of gunpowder, smoke, and death.

The Hawk was on the prowl. From the barracks window, Trueblood saw the inspection party approaching and sang out. They strode down the boardwalk, Hawk MacCauley and Captain Conway side by side, Cohen a little behind them.

The Hawk wore a crisp uniform and moved like a Point man, which he was. He carried a riding crop, which he tapped against his polished boots as he strode.

Rothausen's kitchen had been sparkling. Dutch had cleaned the place from top to bottom. He must have given the spiders dust rags, for not even in the tiny crevices behind the stove could the Hawk find anything.

"Not bad," had been MacCauley's only comment. Rothausen's ruddy face had reddened perceptibly at that. Cohen knew that Dutch had spent twenty extra hours on the kitchen and mess hall.

The captain opened the door to the enlisted barracks for MacCauley, while Cohen called out sharply, "Attention."

MacCauley was in no hurry to enter; he ran a finger along the doorsill before doing so.

Conway glanced at Cohen hopefully, and Ben just shrugged. It was Cohen's ass if the barracks was not ready, but it would also reflect on the captain.

The men stood at rigid attention beside their bunks, their thumbs on the seams of their trousers, their chins pressed to their chests.

MacCauley strolled down the aisle, glancing left and right. He seemed unconcerned with it all, but he hadn't even begun.

Trueblood and Kip Shoendienst were the last men, and it was there that Hawk MacCauley started doing his stuff. He peered at Trueblood's shave as if he wanted to crawl inside his skin, leaned over close enough to his boots to see his own reflection, and then slowly circled Trueblood.

When he gave Schoendienst the same treatment, the kid almost came apart. His lip trembled and his watery eyes seemed to plead.

"What's your name, Private?" MacCauley demanded.

"Schoendienst . . . sir. Schoendienst."

MacCauley had seen men tremble before his eye before, but he had never seen such abject misery. He glanced at Warner Conway. The captain nodded, and MacCauley looked more closely at Schoendienst—if that was possible—and recognized what he saw: a frightened, uncertain farm boy who was facing ten years in prison for a night's foolishness.

Unexpectedly, Hawk MacCauley lifted a hand and rested it briefly on Schoendienst's shoulder. Then he turned and continued.

He examined every bed, searching for holes, stains, and unraveling, which he fully expected to find. Through checking the records of the quartermaster, MacCauley knew exactly how long it had been since Outpost Number Nine had received new material; so MacCauley was able to know just how much of an effort had been made for the sake of this inspection. Despite his reputation, which he nurtured, MacCauley knew damned well that there were only so many ways to make worn old equipment look decent, and he didn't press the field outfits as hard as he did those with a ready access to QM.

This was astonishing. The boots all seemed new and well polished, the beds made up with fresh blankets. The rifles, of course, were use-worn, but he found only a single weapon with so much as a grain of sand in it.

He paused before the bugler and gave him the once-over. Remembering him from Regiment, he said, "McBride, isn't it?"

"Yes, sir, McBride."

MacCauley decided to do McBride up right, and he did. His uniform was new, unwrinkled. His hair was trimmed, his shave close. His bunk was taut, made with new blankets. MacCauley frowned.

He went to McBride's pack, noticed the new canteen, the tightly packed bedroll, the worn but well-cared-for canvas harness. He then opened McBride's locker and nudged the contents with his riding crop.

Spare campaign hat, spare gunbelt and revolver. Bugle case and three starched shirts. MacCauley was growing dissatisfied. His reputation demanded that he find something to disapprove of, but he was damned if he could find anything in McBride's truck.

He stepped back before McBride, who still had his eyes straight forward, chest thrown out, stomach in. "Good looking soldier," he said with a touch of regret.

Then he glanced down, and back to McBride's face. Slowly, MacCauley glanced down again. Damn, the man had big feet! He saw what had to be at least size-twelve boots attached to what could only be a size-nine body, and he smiled despite himself.

MacCauley proceeded to the next man's area, going more rapidly now. The bedroll was as neat as McBride's, which had been nearly perfect. A neat cylinder containing groundsheet, blankets, spare socks and underwear and toilet articles, it was without lump, bump, or stain. MacCauley let his eyes shift slowly back toward McBride's area, and he nodded.

McBride's gear was gone. It had miraculously shifted to this bunk. MacCauley walked slowly to the next bunk, and this time, from the corner of his eye, he saw the roll picked up and passed behind the backs of the soldiers.

It was no new trick, but it went against the Hawk's grain to let them get away with it. The man before him was standing confidently as the major went through his locker, gave him a close personal inspection, and then, glancing at the roll beside the bed, turned and growled.

"That damned bedroll of yours is a mess, Private. A disgrace to the army, a disgrace to you and your sergeant. Get some of these other men to show you how *they* make a decent pack-up!"

Satisfied, Hawk MacCauley buzzed toward the door,

Captain Conway behind him. Cohen lagged behind long enough to give the thumbs-up sign to the barracks.

On the boardwalk, the major confirmed Ben Cohen's feeling. "Damned good, Sergeant. And, I am compelled to add, damned ingenious. I don't know how you did it, really."

"Thank you, sir," Cohen responded.

"I'll talk to the boys at Quartermaster, Warner," the Hawk said. "They seem to have the idea that the people in the field who actually use their equipment are the last ones who should be supplied."

"Thank you, Peter. We do have a hell of a time getting our requests through channels."

"I know you do, it's—"

Major MacCauley's sentence was interrupted by the arrival of the patrol. Riding through the gates with Sergeant Olsen at the point, they looked weary and grim.

It was a moment before Conway reacted to it, then it came suddenly, starkly clear.

That fine white gelding was walking stiffly, its flank stained with dried blood, and across the saddle there was a body. The body of John Fairchild, Jr. Warner Conway's heart sank. He saluted briefly.

"If you'll excuse me, Peter. Looks like serious trouble."

"Of course." MacCauley snapped a salute and Conway stepped off the boardwalk, striding toward a waiting Windy Mandalian and Gus Olsen.

Private Armstrong was leading his horse past, and Ben called, "What happened?"

"We squabbled with some Arapaho, Sergeant. Lieutenant Fairchild, he's dead."

"Damn." Cohen had forgotten Hawk MacCauley. Now, from the corner of his eye, Cohen saw that MacCauley was mounting his horse.

"Sergeant Cohen?"

"Yes, sir?"

Cohen spun that way. MacCauley was stiff in the saddle, his face expressionless. He nodded toward Captain Conway, who was seeing to the body of Lieutenant Fairchild, listening as Windy and Olsen sketched out the episode for him.

"The captain's got other things on his mind just now. I don't want to rush him on his report. Maybe," MacCauley suggested, "you could answer a couple of questions for me, Sergeant Cohen, so that I'll be able to fill in the situation for the TJA."

"Sir?" Cohen's eyes narrowed.

"That patrol." MacCauley nodded his head. "Perhaps I'm wrong, but wasn't that young deserter, Schoendienst, out with them?"

"He could have been, sir," Cohen said warily. What was up? "He certainly could have been," Cohen repeated.

"And am I mistaken—you'll have to ask the captain, of course—or didn't the young man perform gallantly in the skirmish? One might say . . . with heroism enough to redeem himself?"

"Why, I'd have to check with the captain, sir," Cohen said, fighting back a smile of relief, "but the major could be perfectly correct. I am sure that Captain Conway will remark on any such extenuating circumstance in his report on Private Schoendienst."

"I am sure he will," MacCauley answered. He leaned back in his saddle, expressionless as ever, his eyes flat and dark. "I'll let the TJA know that we probably have a case of redemption through valor here."

"I am sure the captain will appreciate your trouble, sir."

Cohen saluted, and it was a smart salute, one that MacCauley returned with never a wink, never a smile. "No trouble, Sergeant. None at all. We're all army, after all."

With that, MacCauley turned his horse and, his two assistants at his flanks, rode at a walk past the dismounted patrol and out through Outpost Number Nine's open gate.

thirteen ─────────────

It was three o'clock on a Wednesday afternoon when Matt Kincaid rode his horse across the broad, shallow Canadian River and onto the Darlington Agency land, his soldiers and forty Cheyenne Indians behind him.

It was a dusty, dry day, and the few scattered oaks drooped, bowing to the heat of the sun. There were tipis here and there, jerry-built shelters of discarded wood and tarpaper, a few brush shelters. From these, curious eyes looked out to watch the passing of the Cheyenne under the Easy Company escort.

It was six miles to the agency buildings: a stockade, a general store, a smithy, a warehouse, and a group of offices set behind high stake walls. Blanket Indians loafed in the shade. As Kincaid and Dancing Horse rode into the agency grounds, dogs yapped at the heels of their horses.

Two blue-uniformed Indian police stood watching from hooded eyes.

"We will be our own police?" Dancing Horse asked.

"That's the way they've set it up, Dancing Horse."

That seemed important to him, and he nodded with satisfaction.

"You wouldn't want the army watching you, would you?"

"No. Not unless it was your army, Kincaid," Dancing Horse replied.

The police they saw were Cherokee, but also on the

reservation they had seen Sioux, Cheyenne, Arapaho, and Creek.

Matt Kincaid nodded to the policemen, who, aware and proud of their new positions of authority, hardly bobbed their heads in response.

Walking into the agency office, the first sight they saw was a white doctor and an Indian nurse, tending to a man with a broken arm. Beyond them, a line of women had formed up before the desk of a harried, white-dressed Cherokee man of twenty or so.

The Cherokee, astonishingly to Dancing Horse, had his hair cropped short and brushed back. He wore a dark suit, stiff collar, and spectacles.

"So that is the new way," Dancing Horse said without inflection.

"One way." Matt added, "It will be good for your people. They will survive and prosper. You have led them well."

Dancing Horse said nothing, but he looked unconvinced. Matt Kincaid himself was not convinced. Reporting to a secretary, a balding white man with sun-reddened skin, they had only a five-minute wait before they were admitted to the Indian agent's office.

He took Kincaid's report—a condensed and expurgated version of the events of the long march—and shook his hand. Then Matt handed over his receipts for supplies purchased, was given a draft to hand over to the secretary, and was bade good day.

It was concluded that quickly. Dancing Horse sat with the agent and they spoke of regulations, supplies, campsites, schools, and the future.

Kincaid exchanged his draft for gold, which the secretary extracted from a barrel safe in the floor behind his desk, and then the lieutenant stepped out onto the porch. The sun was bright in his eyes. The Indian policemen, arms folded, watched him without interest as he stepped down and mounted his horse.

He rode out through the gate and past the Cheyenne, who

154

sat on the grass, looking around them with wooden expressions.

Iron Owl sat his pony to one side, his two scouts with him. Matt thanked them for a good job and paid them off, and then they too were gone, riding slowly northward.

Easy Company had bivouacked half a mile farther on, among some great oaks along a dry creekbed. Wojensky was waiting when Matt swung down beside his tent.

"Done, sir?"

"Done." Matt looked over his camp. He told Wojensky, "They've got beer and whiskey at the agency sutler's. We'll let the boys have one night to howl—they deserve it. Will you watch Malone?"

"I'll watch him like a hawk, sir, like a hawk. For the men, thank you." Wojensky saluted and turned away, spreading the good news among the soldiers, who were set into immediate motion. He heard them laughing and shouting, and he smiled faintly, hoping they could stay out of trouble for one evening.

Kincaid himself walked into his tent and stripped, then washed the trail grime from his body. He shaved, shook out a shirt that was at least fresher than the one he had on, and strapped his gunbelt back on.

Back outside, he observed that the camp was already nearly empty. Holzer, his uniform nearly as immaculate as it had been the day they had left Outpost Number Nine, was being exhorted to haste by Malone. They rode past Kincaid in a minute, snapping salutes, which Matt returned.

And then he was alone in an empty camp. He had no urge for whiskey or companionship just then. He walked along the bank of the dry river, his boots sinking deeply into the sand beneath the cottonwoods.

Frogs grumbled somewhere upriver, and cicadas hummed in the willow brush. The shadows were lengthening, and the tips of the trees were lighted with dusky purples and reds. Matt turned back, watching two mockingbirds at play in one of the dark oaks.

155

He planned to have a quick meal of tinned beef and then stretch out for a long, long night's rest. For the first time in three weeks, there seemed no possibility of his being unexpectedly disturbed.

But then he walked into the shadowed camp and saw the appaloosa pony ground-tethered beside his own horse. Frowning, Matt walked to his tent, swung open the flap, and stepped in to face her.

"Lieutenant," she said in greeting.

"Jenny."

Her hair flowed loose down her back, her eyes were wide and almost childlike as she surveyed Matt Kincaid. Her generous mouth formed a bittersweet expression. She was uneasy, obviously. There was some undefined, electric emotion just beneath the surface; it shone in her eyes.

"What can I do for you?" Matt asked.

"Nothing, I just came to apologize."

"Apologize?"

"Yes." She stepped nearer to him, and Matt could smell the powder and soap mingled with the earthy, underlying scent of a woman. "I was wrong, I treated you scornfully. I thought I was doing right to stand by my—the colonel." She turned her eyes down. "But I was wrong. He was wrong. Perhaps his mind . . ."

She looked up again, and now those big eyes were filled with tears. She shuddered and then stepped into his arms, her shoulders rolling with her sobbing. He held her lightly.

"I am so sorry," she said. Then Jenny turned her mouth to his. He tasted the tears with her kiss. Outside, it was nearly dark, inside the tent it was darker yet, and when Jenny stepped quickly out of his arms, it was a moment before he realized why she had done so.

"Matt?"

"Still here," he answered.

Then she was in his arms again, but when he embraced her, his hands found smooth, bare flesh. Her dress lay on the floor behind her, and as she pressed herself against Matt Kincaid, her fingers worked frantically, unbuttoning his

156

tunic. Her hands slipped inside his tunic and she held him tightly.

This was an emotional woman under a deal of strain, and Matt debated with himself. She was offering, eagerly offering, but would it end in tears, anger, frustration? Her hands dropped to his trousers and she unbuttoned them, her lips locking onto his as she murmured pleasurably and her hands sought for and found his shaft, which wriggled and flooded with blood, growing in her hands.

The debate ended in a rush of emotion, and Matt stripped off his tunic and kicked off his boots as she urged him to hurry.

Naked, he followed her to the cot, pausing only to drop the tent flap. She was warm beneath him, her breasts soft and even more ample than he had thought, and his hand, dropping between the smoothness of her thighs, found her warm, eagerly willing.

"Love me now," she whispered. "Don't wait." And she spread her knees, clutching at his member, centering it, taking him inside her warm depths.

She rolled beneath him. Her breath was moist, warm against his ear, her body fluid and exacting beneath him. Matt clung to her, nuzzling her breasts, clutching her white, firm buttocks as he sunk himself to the hilt, trembling.

"More. Harder. More," she breathed, and he accommodated her. Her legs lifted, spread, and wrapped around his waist as she bucked furiously against him.

He was deep in sensual concentration, and it was a wonder he saw it, but he did. She writhed and swayed beneath him, bringing him to the brink of climax, but it flashed silver in her hand, and he saw it arcing downward, and he rolled away.

The knife just grazed his shoulder, but it filled him with searing pain and he scrabbled from the bed, breaking the grip of her legs.

"You bastard!" she panted, and her voice was a low growl. "You murdering bastard. You killed him! You son of a bitch, you killed my man!" She moved across the

157

darkened tent. Matt dipped away from another cut with the knife.

He could see her now, hair in her eyes, naked breasts swaying, knife glittering in her hand. His own breath was coming raggedly. His shoulder was on fire, and blood dribbled down his arm to splatter against the floor.

"I thought he was your father," Matt said. He was trying to distract her as he circled toward the canvas chair where his gunbelt rested.

"My father. My man..." she panted heavily, then lunged. He slapped her aside. He grabbed at her knife hand as she fell, but missed.

"Kill him. Kill him!" Jenny screamed, and Matt thought she had gone mad until he saw the dark figure in the doorway. "Kill him, Jacklin!"

Jacklin planned on doing just that. Even in the near-darkness, Matt could see the big blue Colt in his hand, the vicious smile on his lips. As he brought his gun up, Matt dove toward the canvas chair.

Jacklin's gun stabbed flame twice, the bullets whipping past Matt's head. He had his holster in his hand now, and as he rolled aside he brought his pistol up, firing just as Jacklin did.

Jacklin's bullet smashed into his pack, lifting it from the floor. Matt's answering shot did not miss.

Jacklin was slammed back. He teetered for a second trying to lift his gun again. He went to his tiptoes, wavered, and fell dead against the earth, a strangled gurgling coming from his blood-filled mouth.

Matt turned his gun toward Jenny Chadwick, not knowing if he could shoot her or not.

But she gave him no choice. She lunged, her mad hair flying, her knife flashing toward him, and he pulled the trigger.

She fell, then got to her feet and staggered toward him. A crimson rose appeared above her left breast, spreading downward. Matt drew back the hammer of his revolver again, and waited.

Jenny took another step and her legs buckled. She fell to the earth before him, so near that her hair brushed his bare feet.

He crouched, tearing the knife from her iron grip. Rolling her over, he looked into her eyes, which were open to the cold, cold night, and he knew there was nothing that could be done for her.

He stumbled toward his cot, which still smelled of the living Jenny Chadwick, and sagged to a sitting position, the pistol in his hands dangling between his legs as he breathed deeply, staring at the two crumpled forms.

The pain in his shoulder had somehow been momentarily forgotten. Now it returned with a vengeful rush, and Matt grimaced.

Rising, he stepped into his trousers and lit the lantern. By the dull yellow glare of the lantern, Jenny's white body seemed unbearably dead and hideous. He covered her with a blanket, noticing that even in death her pretty face was contorted with anger and hatred.

He managed to drag her outside, moving Jacklin out beside her. He left them both there, covered with blankets, then returned to the tent, his shoulder throbbing.

He washed the wound, which was deep but clean across the deltoid muscle, then broke into his first-aid pack and found a gauze pad and bandage. He wrapped it as well as possible, tying the knot with his teeth. There was a pint of brandy in the pack as well, and Kincaid drank a tin cup full, dulling the gnawing pain.

Then he lay back on his bunk, his body pulsing, his mind exhausted by the few moments of incredible tension. He slept soundly and did not awaken until shortly before midnight, when he looked up to see Wojensky in the entrance-way.

"What is it, Corporal?"

"Just checked in to let you know everyone is accounted for, sir. We all made it back."

"Fine," Matt said weakly.

"No one hurt, nothing broken," Wojensky went on. He

159

was bright with liquor himself, his voice cheery, eyes animated. "But we had us a damned good time. Sorry you had to miss all the excitement, sir."

"I'm sorry too, Corporal. Fill me in tomorrow, all right?"

"I will," Wojensky promised. Then he saluted—a reckless, carefree salute—and departed, leaving Matt to drowse away the painful, memory-haunted night.

fourteen ─────────────

Fourteen days later, Lieutenant Matt Kincaid led his trail-weary detachment into Outpost Number Nine. The low, colorless, rough outpost was a welcome sight somehow. It was home, and home always looks good to the weary.

Dusting himself off, Matt stopped only to stretch the kinks from his back before he walked stiffly up onto the boardwalk and entered Captain Conway's office to report.

Ben Cohen was behind his desk, and he rose, saluted, and then shook hands warmly.

"Glad to see you back, sir."

"Believe it or not, I'm happy to be back, Sergeant. How did the inspection come off? And how are our newlyweds? Cambury promised to have me to dinner when I got back."

"The inspection came off fine, sir." Cohen's broad face was cheerless. "Maybe you'd better let the captain fill you in on the rest of what's happened while you were gone."

Conway did fill him in. He related first the manner in which Cambury's impending marriage was broken up. Matt simply shook his head.

"A damned bad break."

"Maybe it's for the best, Matt, I honestly don't know. The girl wasn't cut out for frontier life. Anyway," he said, taking a deep breath, "it appears Mr. Cambury may have another shot at it."

"Sir?"

"He's requested a transfer, and I'm inclined to let him

go. He wants to go East—and I don't have to meditate too deeply to understand why. He's got Pamela Drake on his mind. He's lost the enthusiasm he once had. Probably it would be best for the army if he was sent where he would be happy."

"I wish him the best."

"So do I," Captain Conway said. He rose and got two glasses from his cupboard. Extracting the half-empty bottle of bourbon from his bottom desk drawer, he poured himself and Kincaid a drink. From across the parade echoed the voice of Gus Olsen, drilling his platoon.

"Then what about Mr. Fairchild, sir?" Kincaid asked. "What do you plan to do about him?"

"Fairchild is dead, Matt."

Matt looked up in surprise. He listened while Conway told him about the quick, useless battle with the Arapaho.

"He wouldn't listen to Windy, he wouldn't listen to Olsen. He asked for it, Matt, and he got it. The kid was just no damned good. It's difficult for me to accept. His father is a hell of a man, a hell of a soldier."

"What did you do?"

"What could I do? I wrote John Fairchild a letter and told him that his son had died bravely in battle."

Conway was silent then, and Matt sipped his whiskey, watching the captain, who shook off his troubled thoughts after a moment, and smiled.

"It's a funny thing, Matt, but that useless firefight with the Arapahos produced two heroes for us: John Fairchild, Jr. and Kip Schoendienst."

"Schoendienst?" Matt was perplexed. "I thought he was standing in the shadow of the hangman's noose."

"I'm afraid he was, before he redeemed himself in that run-in." Conway had a sly smile on his lips; refilling Kincaid's glass, he told him about Hawk MacCauley's discreet suggestion.

"So the Hawk has a heart."

"So it seems. Surprising, isn't it?" Conway continued.

"There was another curious episode that took place about the same time as that inspection. Pop Evans burst in here waving his arms, shrieking that someone had broken into his store while he was gone."

"Gone? Gone where?"

"He didn't say. I've an idea that he was dealing somewhere he's not supposed to; you might ask Cohen about that. I've a suspicion that our first shirt knows more about it than he's told me. All I know is that Evans was incensed. He kept saying, 'There weren't even any damned furs.'"

"What was his complaint, sir?"

"It seems that someone had gotten into his store and for some reason moved all his goods to the wrong shelves. Inexplicable, actually." Conway smiled briefly. "Nothing was missing, so there was nothing I could do. He still rants about it, given half a chance. But now, Matt, you'll have to tell me about that Oklahoma Trail. No problems, I hope."

It was Kincaid's turn to smile ruefully. He told his story from the beginning, and without leaving out an eventful moment. His voice was low, and as he got to the end of his story, it was charged with emotion.

They simply sat there for a time, facing each other across Captain Conway's desk, and then Conway said, "Well, it's over. Bury it, Matt, like you buried them. There's nothing else to be done. You will write it up?"

"I'll write it up. It won't be easy, but I'll write it up."

They rose together. Conway walked him to the door, telling him, "If your shoulder's still bothering you, take a day or two off. We can get along."

"I'd just as soon get back into the swing of things, sir, if you don't mind."

"All right. Maybe that is best. Dinner with Flora and me tonight?" the captain asked with a warm smile.

"There's nothing I'd like better, sir."

"Seven o'clock?"

"Seven it is, sir."

And then Conway was gone. Matt Kincaid stood alone

163

for a long while on the boardwalk. He looked past the parade, where Olsen had finished drilling his men, past the tall gates.

It was a clear, windless afternoon, and he could see an incredible distance across the long grass plains. For a moment, standing quietly, looking across the prairie, it was almost as if he could see all the way to the bitter, distant end of that Oklahoma Trail.

SPECIAL PREVIEW

Here are the opening scenes
from

EASY COMPANY AND THE CHEROKEE BEAUTY

the next novel in Jove's exciting
High Plains adventure series

EASY COMPANY

coming in March!

one ━━━━━━━━━━━━━━━━━

The wind was hard out of the north. The long grass trembled before it. There was new spring grass now, after the recent rains, showing brilliant green in patches interspersed with the older, brown grass, much of which had been flattened by weather and buffalo. The wind clutched at an old broken cottonwood and throttled it. A dust devil, picked up on a barren knoll, was swept across the plains and dropped nearly in front of Lieutenant Fitzgerald's chunky, deep-chested bay.

He closed his eyes tightly against the dust. Then he wiped the sweat from his forehead and turned in the saddle to study the rest of his detachment briefly. The sun was in their eyes, and it was still a hot sun, and the men rode with their hats low, squinting into the yellow heat of the day.

He was aware suddenly of Gus Olsen moving up beside him. The platoon sergeant wore an expression of concern mixed with his usual affability.

"Got scouts coming in, Lieutenant," Olsen said, and Fitzgerald's eyes followed the stubby pointing finger to the north, where Windy Mandalian's appaloosa stood out against the dry grass plains. Behind Windy and slightly to the west was Joseph Hatchet, the Delaware scout. Neither man was trying to make time. They alternately walked and loped their ponies toward the detachment, which plodded westward, enveloped in yellow dust clouds of its own making.

"Looks like they've got nothing to report," Fitzgerald said, more to himself than to Olsen.

"Nothin' urgent," Gus agreed.

Fitzgerald glanced again at the sun, and frowned. They were a good fifteen miles out, and he was beginning to grow uneasy about this expedition. They were far enough from Outpost Number Nine to be cut off if that damned Wraps-Up-His-Tail had as many warriors as the "moccasin telegraph" had reported.

"Keep your eyes open for a campsite, Sergeant," Fitzgerald said. "Darkness will be coming up on us real quick."

Olsen nodded and let his horse fall back behind the lieutenant's. Windy was nearly to the point of the column now, Hatchet still a quarter of a mile off.

Fitzgerald took a deep drink from his canteen and sighed, watching Windy trail in. Wraps-Up-His-Tail was out here somewhere. The Crow had been spotted by Chase, one of Windy's informants, and the word passed on by runner. He hadn't had time to break camp, or at least Fitzgerald doubted it. The moccasin telegraph moved quickly. When Matt Carrol of the Diamond D bull trains was asked to ride from General Crook's headquarters on the Rosebud to carry news of the Little Big Horn disaster north to Fort Keogh, a trip that took the hard-riding Carrol three days, he found out that the Indians around the fort had gotten news of the battle the day before he arrived.

"You're coming in damn slow these days," Fitzgerald told Windy as the scout pulled in behind him. Windy shook his head and spat a stream of tobacco juice, wiping his lips with his sleeve.

"Yes," Windy drawled, "and if you see me comin' in quick, you'd best have these boys unlimber their guns."

"You didn't see anything?" He looked at Hatchet. The Delaware apparently had nothing to report, either.

"No sign of Mr. Lo," Windy answered. He took off his flop hat and wiped back his long, thinning hair. "Old Chase, he knew exactly where they was. But this area is crisscrossed by draws and coulees, Lieutenant. Now an Indian like

Chase, he's lived here all his life and he knows where the second buffalo wallow up the coulee by the big trees is, could find it on a dark night in his sleep. Me, I've a good notion where the damned Crow is supposed to be, but it'll take a little scouting."

"Just so we find him before he gets too eager to show his stuff."

Windy nodded agreement and swung out to talk to Joseph Hatchet. The Delaware had seen nothing, but his pony had pulled up lame.

Fitzgerald watched the endless prairie, where, in the far distance, the Rockies showed as a low, nearly purple line against the dun brown of the horizon, and he silently cursed. He could have been in Kansas City. They were due for furlough, all of them.

Captain Conway was gone to Denver to spend some time in a soft bed with Flora, and with any luck they would eventually get a summer relief officer to Outpost Number Nine, but in the meantime it was grinding. The outpost was habitually undermanned, and now the only officers were Taylor, Kincaid, and Fitzgerald, all of them itching for furlough.

"I think we might want to camp on that knoll, Lieutenant," Sergeant Olsen said. Fitzgerald hadn't even noticed the big man riding up beside him. He glanced at the low knoll where a half-dozen big oaks stood, shuddering in the wind, then turned to look at his detachment; the men were dusty, weary, purpled by the sundown light.

"All right," he agreed. "Post a double guard, Sergeant."

"I was intendin' to, sir," Olsen answered. "What about a fire?"

"Only until dark. I don't suppose a fire could show any farther than this dust we're kicking up."

They made camp beneath the oaks, watching the crimson fire of the sun extinguish itself while coffee boiled. The bedrolls were already rolled out, and several soldiers, exhausted by the day in the saddle beneath the hot sun, were already snoring.

The night guards ate first and were given coffee, then they spread out, filtering throuth the shadows toward their assigned posts.

At full dark, Olsen ordered dirt thrown onto the fire, and that triggered a lot of grumbling. Dillson was the loudest complainer, as he was the loudest complainer about everything from the red ants on the ground beneath the oaks to the strength of the coffee.

"If the scouts can't find no Injuns, then they're damn sure too far off to see a fire."

"Not at night, Dillson," Gus Olsen told him. "Use your head."

"It's bullshit," Dillson muttered, leaning back against the rough trunk of an oak. "Matter of fact, this is the most bullshit outfit I've ever been hooked up with."

Reb McBride glanced up from his coffee and said without a smile, "It sure as hell is since you showed up, Dillson."

Olsen sighed and walked away. There was no way short of beating Dillson to death to shut him up. Gus knew, he had tried. So had Ben Cohen, and when Cohen couldn't handle a man, the man was a lost cause.

Not that he wasn't a good soldier; Dillson was—or could have been. But he had been in the artillery before, and hated everything that wasn't artillery. If they'd let him, Dillson would be walking around in those redleg pants he'd brought with him.

Cohen was trying to get him back to artillery, but it wasn't easy. Apparently, Dillson hadn't been too well loved even there. Dillson watched Olsen walk away to sit beside the now-cold fire on a rotten log.

"Still bullshit," Dillson mumbled.

"I don't want to risk my hide on it," Reb told him. "Besides, it's an order. Don't you artillery boys take orders?"

"Damn right we do," Dillson flared up. "But in artillery you've got good noncoms, good officers."

"Gus Olsen is one of the best there is," Rafferty said from behind his forward-tilted hat.

"Bullshit."

They sat there in silence for a while, the only sounds the humming of mouse-sized mosquitoes, the occasional slap of a hand against someone's neck in retaliation.

"Who the hell is this Wraps-Up-His-Tail anyway?" Dillson asked.

"Just a hostile," Rafferty said, his voice broken by a yawn. "Damned renegade Crow is what he is."

"Crow!" Dillson snorted. "They worried about a Crow gettin' these Cheyenne and Plains Sioux together?" He laughed, his mouth hanging open stupidly. Dillson was an ox of a man, almighty thick through the chest and shoulders. The bulk of his body was sheathed in extra meat, and even his face was excessively heavy, with bulldog pouches on his cheeks.

"He's got big medicine," Reb McBride said, rolling over onto his side, his head propped up on his hand. "Way Windy heard it from Chase, the man's claimin' he can make himself invisible."

"Why, he could be out there right now!" Dillson said with mock horror. Then he laughed again. "Them Injuns'll swallow anything, won't they?"

"They're desperate, I reckon," Reb said. "A white man swallows just as much garbage. But a man comes up to these men and tells 'em he can defeat the army—why, there's always a few ready to give it a try."

"I heard," Rafferty put in, "that Wraps-Up-His-Tail is sayin' he can kill a man with a knife at a mile just by pointing it at him. It's big medicine, and there's always a few malcontents, braves who've been run off from their own tribes, kids wanting to earn their feathers to follow a medicine man who promises to make 'em strong."

For Dillson, who had asked the question in the first place, the explanation was too long. He was already snoring. The question had arisen from his complaining, but he really had no interest in the Crow medicine man; when it was time to fight, he would fight. Now it was time to sleep, and he did that as greedily and noisily as he did everything else, his great slack jaws quivering as he rumbled a snore.

"Listen to that," Rafferty said with a grimace.

"Yeah," Reb responded. "Thank God he's a likable son of a bitch otherwise."

"You know, Reb, one of us could just walk over there and slit his damned throat for him. Blame it on the hostiles."

"Could," Reb agreed. "But hell, he probably *bleeds* noisy."

Rafferty chuckled and rolled up in his blankets, and Reb did the same, tugging his blanket up around his ears.

They moved out at first light, riding westward in a picket line, with Windy Mandalian and Joseph Hatchet a good mile ahead. There was more new grass as they moved toward the mountains, and a good-sized herd of buffalo grazing placidly to the south. Fitzgerald felt better without the dust, although he still had only a slender hope of coming up unseen on Wraps-Up-His-Tail.

They saw nothing through the long morning except a pair of rail-thin, scavenging wolves working over a buffalo carcass. The wolves loped off as the squad approached, watched with yellow eyes from the long grass, and circled back as they passed.

They cut the Tankford Coulee just before two o'clock, and the soldiers funneled down through a sandy cut into the bottom, which was heavy with budding cottonwood and willow.

There was enough water there for the horses, so Fitzgerald halted them there. It was hot even in the shade. Sweat trickled down his neck. His uniform, which had been fresh upon leaving Number Nine, was white with sweat.

He let his bay drink its fill, and his thoughts inevitably drifted to Kansas City. First the captain would have to get back, but he was due. Then it was Kincaid's turn for furlough—say a month, then. A month in a real hotel bed with silk sheets, cognac, and women in satin ball gowns...

His head came up sharply with the shout, and he yanked his startled bay's head around. The Indian had been lying low in the willows, and now he had decided to make his break for it.

Fitzgerald saw a flash of color on the man's face, the blurred coloring of his roan through the screen of willow. Then the rider swung his pony up the sandy banks of the wash and achieved the flats in a flurry of sand.

"Rafferty! Dillson!" He swung his arm toward the two mounted men nearest him, and they spurred their horses into a run.

Rafferty had seen the Indian nearly at the moment Lieutenant Fitzgerald did, but he was frozen into immobility. When he did move, it was ineffectually, starting his pony, then stopping to grab at his Springfield.

But when Fitzgerald waved his arm, Rafferty heeled his bay forward. He had been told before that he was quicker at following orders than when thinking for himself. Maybe it was true.

Now he splashed his horse across the yard-wide stream and urged him up the sandy bluffs, feeling his horse sink nearly to its haunches as he spurred upward.

The horse scrambled for purchase and then was up, running on the broad flat plains. Rafferty glanced over his shoulder to see Dillson coming up quickly. The big man rode stiff-backed in the saddle, which might have struck Rafferty as funny at another time.

Now his attention was only on the Indian pony ahead of him, and the brave who rode low across its withers. It was a dead-out horse race, and Rafferty knew the bigger army horses would run down the mustang pony. He only hoped, with fleeting panic, that the Indian wasn't leading them into a trap.

He crossed his right hand and drew his Schofield Smith & Wesson, which was holstered on his left side, butt forward, and fired a shot well over the Indian's head, hoping that it might pull him up.

The Indian didn't even look back, which told Rafferty that the man had something to run from. A friendly, perhaps

173

startled by the soldiers, might have taken off. Might have, but he damn sure would have stopped rather than get shot.

The dust plumed out behind Rafferty's horse. The bay was running well, taking long, ground-devouring strides, despite the long trail.

He was closing the gap between himself and the fugitive. Glancing back, Rafferty could see that Dillson was keeping pace, though he was eating a lot of dust.

The Indian was there, and then he wasn't, and Rafferty guided his pony to one side, still at a dead run, knowing the Indian had found a wash and might just leap off his pony's back and fight.

He intended to come up on the wash just a little north of where he was expected to appear. Rafferty hoped Dillson had taken a clue from him and swerved off to the south, but the big man was still in his dust. Rafferty waved a hand, motioning Dillson away. The big man, misunderstanding, slowed his horse instead, and Rafferty cursed.

"Dumb son of a bitch!"

Dillson had never wanted to sit around jawing with the men, and as a result he had learned nothing since arriving at Number Nine. Rafferty cursed his luck for drawing Dillson on this. Reb, Malone, Stretch, or any of them would have swung their horses south, and the result would be that the Indian would be caught between the searchers.

Rafferty saw the wash open up suddenly before him. Steep-walled, fifty feet deep, clotted with cottonwoods and contending brush, it offered what the Indian had been looking for: concealment.

Rafferty slid his bay down the bank, drawing up at the bottom in the dust of his own making, listening to the silence. Cicadas and mosquitoes hummed in the willow brush. Upstream a ways, bullfrogs grumped in the reeds. Rafferty looked back, saw no sign of Dillson, and dismounted, lifting his Springfield from the spider on his saddle.

He moved into the brush, pausing to listen every few

174

steps. It was warm in the wash, shielded from the breeze as he was. He heard no telling sound, saw no movement or patch of color.

He wove through the brush-clotted wash, hands cramped around his Springfield, boots swishing through the sand underfoot. He started a cottontail to running, and his rifle swung that way automatically. Swallowing a tense curse, Rafferty wiped the salt sweat from his eyes and walked on, moving now to a sort of bench from which he had a view of the bottoms. Dillson never did show; Rafferty figured the man was watching to make sure the Indian did not break out onto the flats again.

It was unlikely that the brave would try that, Rafferty thought. He had cover in the wash, and he would know the main body of soldiers would be arriving shortly. Knowing that, the Indian would stick to the bottoms and he would move soon. North or south? That was the only question. Rafferty's eyes scanned the wash. He could see nothing yet, all the way to the big westward bend a half-mile off, and if the Indian had gotten that far, he was a magician. The brush was heavy, and that pony would have to make noise crashing through it.

Rafferty's tongue was dry. His chest was soaked with perspiration, and his shirt clung to it. He squatted down himself, holding his own silence, leaving it to the Indian to make his move.

And then he was there. Bursting out of the willows, his pony leaping over a dead tree, the Indian heeled his paint directly toward Rafferty. Rafferty saw the Indian's arms come up, saw the rifle in his hands, and he threw himself to one side, hearing the explosion, the muffled impact of the bullet into the sand near his head.

A second shot followed on the heels of the first. Still the Indian charged at Rafferty, and Rafferty brought his Springfield around. He could see the paint on the warrior's face clearly: green and yellow on one side of his face. He could even see that the man's nose had once been broken. He heard the pounding of the pony's hoofs, the hard breathing of the wild-eyed horse, and then a shot exploded behind and above him, and he flinched reflexively.

A smear of crimson appeared on the Indian's bare chest, and the horse turned sharply away from Rafferty, who was braced, prepared to dive headlong to one side. The pony heeled around, spraying a shower of dust at Rafferty, and the Indian tumbled from its back.

The body rolled head over heels once, and then stopped dead next to Rafferty as the bucking paint pony lunged downstream through the brush.

Rafferty sat there for a moment, his heart pounding. Not five feet away the Indian lay, faceup. His chest was torn open by a big .45-70 bullet. His heart gave one convulsive leap and then stopped, the blood leaking out to stain the white sand. The Indian, his expression savage even in death, stared into the sun with open, angry eyes.

Rafferty heard a noise behind him and spun around, but it was only Dillson. The big man slid down the bluff in a small avalanche of sand and rocks, landing on his rump beside Rafferty.

Dillson was grinning, rifle held high, and he got to his feet, poking the Indian with a boot toe.

"Saved your ass, I reckon!" he said triumphantly.

"I guess you did," Rafferty had to admit. He too was studying the dead brave. A shadow crossed his face and he glanced up now to see a line of horses against the sky.

"Dead?" Lieutenant Fitzgerald called down.

"Yes, sir!" Rafferty called back, and he heard Fitzgerald breathe a slow, fluent curse. Dillson had his hat off, mopping his forehead.

A line was thrown down, and Rafferty looped the rope under the dead warrior's armpits, then retrieved his bay and heeled it, stumbling, up the precipitous slope. He dismounted and watched as the Indian was dragged up and over.

Windy slid from his appy's saddle and strode over, going to his haunches to study the bloody body. Lieutenant Fitzgerald remained on his horse as Windy stood and announced, "Oglala Sioux." He shook his head. "Ain't a whole lot more to be learned from a dead man, Lieutenant."

"No." Fitzgerald's mouth was compressed into a straight, harsh line. "Damn," he breathed. He had wanted the man alive.

Dillson was just clambering up from out of the gulley, a grin on his bulldog face.

"Rafferty!" the lieutenant shouted, and Rafferty turned that way. "Come here. You too, Dillson."

The big man spat and walked to where Fitzgerald waited, still on horseback. "What happened, Dillson? You know I wanted that man alive."

Dillson's face went beet red and he sputtered before answering: "Sir, he was about to ride Rafferty here down. He had cut his dogs loose and I had to send mine out, else watch Rafferty take it."

"Is that right, Rafferty?" Fitzgerald asked.

"That's the way it was, Lieutenant. That Sioux was just about to bury me."

"All right." Fitzgerald looked away, studying the distances for a moment. The wind flattened the cheat grass, turning it silver. A lone crow circled against a high, brilliant sky.

It was important to have this Sioux runner alive, but he knew that Dillson had no real choice in it. Still, the big man could have tried to drop the Indian's pony, tried to wound him. That shot was dead center.

"That's all, boys," Fitzgerald said. He snapped a half-salute and turned his bay.

"That son of a bitch," Dillson muttered.

"It's just that he wanted the man alive," Rafferty said with a shrug.

Dillson blinked with incomprehension. "And you dead?"

"That's not what he meant," Rafferty told him.

"I save your butt, and you side with him against me!"

"I'm siding with no one, Dillson. I know you pulled me out of the fire back there. I'm just telling you that Fitzgerald

177

didn't mean anything personal by what he said. He's just mad that the thing blew up in our faces."

"He just wanted to walk on somebody," Dillson said angrily. His eyes shuttled to where Fitzgerald, dismounted, stood talking to Windy Mandalian. "Anybody. He's one of them officers that's got to ride somebody, got to prove something to his men."

"Fitzgerald?" Rafferty laughed out loud. Dillson regarded him with a scowl, his dark eyes narrow and hard.

"All of 'em," Dillson said. He spat and turned sulkily toward his horse, still grumbling to himself.

Windy Mandalian had been cogitating, and when the lieutenant swung down beside him, the scout told him what he thought.

"I think this Sioux was a renegade, sir. He's got no reason to be roamin' around this far west by his lonesome, otherwise. I also think I know where he was going when we came up on him."

"Wraps-Up-His-Tail?"

"Yes, sir. Where else? The Crow's the only one we know of who's camped hereabouts. Now I figure this Oglala was either goin' to or comin' from Wraps-Up-His-Tail's camp. Could be I'm wrong, of course, but we got no other leads. If me and old Hatchet take a wide swing back toward the other coulee, we'll likely cut his sign, and while there's still good light, we can track him back and see where he's come from.

"If that don't wash," Mandalian continued, "we'll come back this direction and try to get a line on where he was goin'. The way I see it, one end or t'other will be Wraps-Up-His-Tail's camp."

Fitzgerald couldn't fault the logic of it, and as Mandalian had reminded him, they had no other leads. He sent Windy and Hatchet on back then, glancing at the sun, which was already midway through its descending arc.

Fitzgerald took the opportunity to send a party down into the wash to fill the canteens, which hadn't been filled at the coulee. His eyes settled then on the dusty, blood-caked form of the Sioux, and he called Sergeant Olsen over.

"We need a burial detail, Sergeant."

"Yes, sir." Gus looked at the body, noticing the blue-bottle flies that had already gathered, tracking across the dead man's eyes. "I'll see to it."

"Rafferty and Dillson," Fitzgerald said, not looking at Olsen directly.

"Sir?"

"I want Rafferty and Dillson to bury the man. It's their fault he's lying here."

"Yes, sir," Olsen answered, saluting smartly. It wasn't punishment, exactly, but it would be a reminder to Dillson and Rafferty. Although Dillson was sure to blow his top over this. Gus found the two men sitting in the shade of their horses, drinking from their canteens.

"What's up, Gus?" Rafferty asked.

"Him." He nodded at the corpse. "Lieutenant wants you men to bury him."

"Fuck him," Dillson snarled.

"You better hold it down," Olsen warned him sharply.

"Or what?" he asked challengingly.

"You know damned well what," Olsen said. "This is an order, Dillson. Bury that damned Indian."

Dillson came to his feet heavily, his face livid. "I chased him. I caught him. I shot him before he could kill Rafferty! Now, as thanks, I get to bury the fuckin' savage."

"That's right. Fitzgerald figures he's your responsibility, I guess."

Dillson's jaw was tight. The big man was ready to come unhinged. "I ought to tear him out of that uniform and break his goddamned face for him," he growled.

Reb McBride had wandered over, drawn by the sounds of arguing voices. What he saw was a man at the frayed end of his self-control, standing in front of a wooden Gus Olsen, his dark eyes fixed on Lieutenant Fitzgerald. Reb stepped in, trying to defuse it.

179

"I'll give you a hand, Dillson. Hell, ain't this the army for you? Chickenshit outfit, ain't it?" He pulled the shovel from Dillson's pack and took the big man's arm, grinning and jabbering, but Dillson shook him off.

Olsen had walked away, glancing over his shoulder. Rafferty hissed, "Dammit, Dillson. You don't talk like that about an officer!"

"Talk ain't all I'll do."

"Yeah, and then they'll do *you*. Up against the wall, bang-bang."

"I don't give a shit, Rafferty."

"You will, you will."

"Hit an officer and likely they'll just gun you down here to save you the misery," Reb put in. He could no longer hold the smile on his face. He put his arm on Dillson's shoulder, felt the knot of tensed muscles there, and said gently, "Come on. It's a soldier's life. You know that. Just more bullshit."

"I'm gonna get that son of a bitch," Dillson promised. His eyes lingered on Fitzgerald awhile longer, then he turned angrily away, yanking the shovel out of Reb's hand. Rafferty stood beside the bugler, watching Dillson stalk heavily toward the dead Sioux.

"Thanks, Reb," Rafferty said. His face was pale beneath the coating of yellow dust.

"It's nothin'. Hell of it is, I did it for a man I'd just as soon see shot."

"You and me both," Rafferty agreed, but he knew Reb only half meant it. Dillson was a pain in the butt, but a man sticks up for his partners. Even a redleg. Rafferty snatched up his own shovel and walked off to where Dillson, in a cloud of dust, was furiously shoveling dirt.

Reb watched them both for a minute, then shook his head and walked to his own horse. Stretch Dobbs handed him his reins.

"What's that?" Stretch wanted to know.

"A man headin' for disaster just as fast as he can go," Reb answered.

They drifted slowly westward half an hour later, leaving the Sioux to his gods. The sun was in their eyes; their horses cast long, crooked shadows behind them. They hadn't covered a mile when they saw Mandalian coming in, and he wasn't walking his horse this time—he was riding like hell.

Bestselling Books for Today's Reader — From Jove!

___**CHASING RAINBOWS**   05849-1/$2.95
Esther Sager

___**FIFTH JADE OF HEAVEN**   04628-0/$2.95
Marilyn Granbeck

___**PHOTO FINISH**   05995-1/$2.50
Ngaio Marsh

___**NIGHTWING**   06241-7/$2.95
Martin Cruz Smith

___**THE MASK**   05695-2/$2.95
Owen West

___**SHIKE: TIME OF THE DRAGON**   06586-2/$3.25
(Book 1)
Robert Shea

___**SHIKE: TIME OF THE DRAGON**   06587-0/$3.25
(Book 2)
Robert Shea

___**THE WOMEN'S ROOM**   05933-1/$3.50
Marilyn French

Available at your local bookstore or return this form to:

 **JOVE/BOOK MAILING SERVICE**
P.O. Box 690, Rockville Center, N.Y. 11570

**Please enclose 50¢ for postage and handling for one book, 25¢
each add'l book ($1.25 max.). No cash, CODs or stamps. Total
amount enclosed: $_____ in check or money order.**

NAME_____

ADDRESS_____

CITY_____STATE/ZIP_____
Allow six weeks for delivery.   SK 23